BATTLE BEFORE TIME

Visit the author, Jim Denney, at
www.denneybooks.com/timebenders.html.

TIMEBENDERS

BATTLE BEFORE TIME

JIM DENNEY

www.tommynelson.com

A Division of Thomas Nelson, Inc.
www.ThomasNelson.com

Published in Nashville, Tennessee, by Tommy Nelson®, a Division of Thomas Nelson, Inc.

Unless otherwise noted, Scripture quotations used in this book are from *The Holy Bible, New International Version* (NIV), copyright © 1973, 1978, 1984, by New York International Bible Society, Zondervan Bible Publishers.

Library of Congress Cataloging-in-Publication Data

Denney, James D.
    Battle before time / by Jim Denney.
       p. cm. — (Timebenders #1)
    Summary: A young inventor named Max and three middle school classmates travel back in time to the Garden of Eden where they are tempted by the Enemy to turn away from God.
    ISBN 1-4003-0039-8
    [1. Time travel—Fiction. 2. Inventors—Fiction. 3. Christian life—Fiction.] I. Title.
PZ7.D4272 Bat 2002
[Fic]—dc21   2002016639

Printed in the United States of America

02 03 04 05 06 PHX 5 4 3 2 1

This book is dedicated to Ryan, of course.
(After all, it was his idea!)

CONTENTS

1

WACKY CONTRAPTIONS

"Hey, New Kid! Run faster! Go for the ball!"

Max McCrane groaned as he jogged across the soccer field. *Why do they have to call me New Kid?* he asked himself. *I hate that!*

It was P.E., and Coach Brister had divided the class into two soccer teams, Red and Blue. Max was on the Blue Team. He was trying to lag behind his teammates so no one would kick the ball to him, but that made things worse. "What's the matter, New Kid?" they yelled. "Scared of the ball?"

Max McCrane was your basic, average-looking middle-schooler. Average height and weight. An average-looking face with ordinary brown eyes that were magnified behind the large, round lenses of his glasses. Medium-length hair that was an average shade of brown.

In fact, there was only one thing about Max that *wasn't*

average: his brain. Max was very smart. He wasn't stuck-up about it—not at all. Max just figured *everybody* knows how long it takes light to travel from the sun to the earth (eight minutes and eighteen seconds), or which dinosaurs lived in which era—Triassic, Jurassic, or Cretaceous. So, even though strange things always happened to Max because he was smart, he saw himself as, well, average.

"Hey, New Kid, get in position! Move up on the goal!" yelled Grady Stubblefield, captain of the Blue Team. Grady was a lean, athletic African-American. He had sleek black skin and powerful, cordlike muscles. Grady was always yelling orders—"Work the ball outside!" or "Spread out the field!"—whatever that meant. Max didn't like Grady. He didn't like bossy people who yelled a lot.

Looking left, Max saw Allie O'Dell coming up the sideline. Her carrot-red ponytail bobbed along behind her as she controlled the ball with a series of stutter kicks.

Max frowned. Everybody else in his class seemed to enjoy soccer. Even girls like Allie seemed to enjoy it. But Max *hated* soccer. It wasn't that he was slow or uncoordinated. But kicking a ball into a net? It just seemed so pointless.

Max watched as Allie faked a goal-shot, then side-kicked the ball to Grady. Max was relieved—nobody kicked the ball to him. Grady walloped the ball toward the goal. The Red Team goalie dived and tipped it with outstretched fingers. The ball was deflected away—no score.

"Oh, no," Max groaned. The ball was bouncing right to him.

"Get the rebound, New Kid!" shouted Grady.

New Kid! Max gritted his teeth and tried to trap the ball with his feet. At the same time, he saw a big blur coming at him from the edge of his vision. Max glanced up to see Toby Brubaker, captain of the Red Team, chugging toward him like a freight train. Toby was a mean-looking boy with a butch haircut, pug nose, and little pale green eyes. A vicious sneer twisted his pale, doughy face.

Oh, no, Max thought. *This is going to hurt!*

Toby launched a vicious kick, whacking Max in the right shin. The impact flipped Max facedown onto the grass. Laughing, Toby stole the ball and kept going.

Max's leg screamed with pain. He raised his head and looked over to the sideline where Coach Brister stood. The coach was supposed to referee the game, but his back was turned while he chatted with the principal, Mr. Flammery. *The story of my life,* Max thought. *Grownups are never looking when I get clobbered.*

Grady Stubblefield ran past Max. "Get up, Loser!" he yelled. "They're going to score!"

Wincing, Max clambered to his feet and limped after Grady—too late. Toby Brubaker controlled the ball straight up the middle. Guarding the net was Salina Chavez, Blue Team's goalie. Her dark eyes widened with terror as Toby came at her like a torpedo. Thirty feet from the goal, Toby kicked the ball at the frightened goalie's head. Salina dropped to the ground with a shriek, covering her short brown hair with her hands.

The ball streaked into the net for a Red Team goal. The game was tied, 3 to 3.

Grady flew into a rage. He screamed at Max for letting Toby get the ball. Then he screamed at Salina Chavez for not defending the goal.

"Stubblefield," Coach Brister called from the sideline, "give that mouth of yours a rest—unless you want to spend the rest of the period doing push-ups!" Then he returned to his chat with the principal.

Grady frowned and placed the ball on the center line and kicked off. A boy on Max's team fielded the ball, dribbling it up the middle until he found his way blocked by Toby Brubaker. Toby moved in and gave him a hard bump, but the boy got the ball away to Allie O'Dell. Allie moved the ball twenty yards upfield, then found herself blocked by Red defenders.

Max limped up the field, mentally pleading, *Please, don't kick it to me!* But Allie *did* kick it to Max. To his horror the ball was bounding straight toward him.

Max eyed the goal. The Red Team goalie was out of position and the net was wide open. *If only my leg wasn't throbbing,* Max thought.

The next few seconds passed in slow motion. Max trapped the ball with his right foot. *Ow!* Wincing, he pulled his foot back to kick. Pain lanced from his shin, through his knee, and into his thigh. Grimacing, Max launched his foot with all his might and—

Whiff!

—missed the ball completely!

He put so much force into the kick that he completely upended himself and landed on his back. The wind was knocked out of him.

Laughing insanely, Toby Brubaker swooped in and kicked the ball upfield to one of his teammates. The Red Team player booted the ball past Salina Chavez for the score. Coach Brister blew his whistle, signaling the end of the game.

Final score: Red Team, 4; Blue Team, 3.

Grady Stubblefield came over to where Max lay in the grass. He towered over Max, blocking out the sky. "Nice going, Loser," he snarled, shaking his fist in Max's face. "You cost us the game!"

"I didn't ask to be on your stupid team," Max wheezed, staring cross-eyed at that fist. Max had only been in two fights in his life—and he had lost both of them. He had no doubt that Grady Stubblefield could beat him to a pulp.

Grady turned and stamped away.

Flat on his back, with pain pulsing in his leg and a hot flush of shame in his cheeks, Max became furious. He didn't like being called Loser. He didn't like feeling clumsy and dorky—and he *hated* feeling scared. For a moment, Max's anger won out over his fear. He scrambled to his feet and shouted, "Hey, Stubblefield!"

Grady Stubblefield stopped in his tracks.

"Don't call me Loser," Max wheezed. He tried to sound tough, but his voice was more of a squeak than a roar.

Grady turned, fists clenched. "Are *you* talking to *me,* New Kid?"

Max felt the fear returning—but he was in too deep to back down. "Yeah, I'm talking to you," he gasped. "And don't call me New Kid. My name is Max McCrane!"

Grady walked up and jabbed his finger in Max's chest. "Look," he said, "I don't care if your name is Ronald McDonald! If you ever talk to me that way again, I'll rearrange your face!" Then he turned and walked away.

Max took a deep breath and realized he was wheezing. He took his asthma inhaler out of his pocket and took a puff. *What was I thinking?* he wondered to himself. *That guy could've killed me!*

"Don't let him bother you, Max," said a girl's voice behind him.

Max turned. It was red-haired, freckle-faced Allie O'Dell. Max quickly hid the inhaler in his pocket.

"Grady acts all bossy," she continued, "but he's not really a bad kid."

"You called me Max," he said, amazed.

Allie flashed a friendly grin, revealing a mouth wired with braces. "That's your name, isn't it?"

"Yeah," Max said, "but I've been at this school for a

whole week and everybody still calls me New Kid. Nobody even says 'Hi' to me."

"Well, you and I have two classes together—P.E. and science," Allie said. "It's about time we said 'Hi.' So how do you like it here at Appleton?"

He looked around the schoolyard, thinking how much Victor Appleton Middle School looked like his last school: the same rows of stucco-walled classrooms, painted the same ugly pinkish-tan. The same blacktop basketball courts. He shrugged. "School is school, I guess."

"It's hard to break in at a new school," Allie said. "But don't sweat it, Max—you'll make friends." She smiled a glittering metal smile. "So, like, where did you move from?"

"I didn't move," Max replied. "I've lived in the same house all my life."

"Then why change schools?" Allie asked.

"After the gymnasium sank into the ground," Max said, "my mom and dad thought I'd do better in a different school."

"After the gymnasium sank?" A look of realization dawned on Allie's face. "Whoa! Don't tell me! *You're* the kid who wrecked the gymnasium at Debockel Middle School?"

"Well, now you know," Max said in a hushed voice. "But don't tell anyone, okay? I had to transfer here because people kept razzing me about it at the other school. My parents thought I could get a fresh start here at Victor Appleton."

"Okay, Max," Allie said. "I promise—I won't tell a soul. Just tell me how you wrecked the gym."

"I *didn't* wreck it," Max said defensively. "Not completely, anyway. The gym only sank three feet into the ground—and besides, I didn't do it! My Diggerbot did it."

"What's a Diggerbot?"

"Something I invented—a little robot that digs holes in the ground. I built it as a project in science class, and I took it outside to show my teacher. It was supposed to dig a hole—just one little hole! But when I turned it on, the switch got stuck and it just kept digging! It tunneled under the gym and it kept going around and around!"

"Couldn't anybody stop it?" Allie asked.

"Stop it how?" Max said. "It was tunneling way underground, and it just kept tunneling until the batteries ran down. The principal came out and started yelling and jumping up and down. Then someone called the fire department, and all the firemen could do was tell everybody to keep back."

"Then what?" Allie asked, her eyes big.

"Whump!" Max said, making an all-fall-down gesture with both hands. "The gym sank into a big hole. I don't mean to cause trouble—I just like to invent stuff. But whenever I invent something, trouble just kind of happens."

Allie laughed. "I wish I could've seen the look on your teacher's face when—"

She was interrupted by a clanging bell.

"There's the first bell," Allie said. "We'd better get to science class."

"My backpack's in my locker," Max said, taking off. "See you there."

Allie walked into class with a minute to spare. Around the room, students were settling into their seats or pulling homework out of backpacks. Allie took her place at a table next to Grady Stubblefield. Looking over her shoulder, she checked the door, hoping Max wouldn't be late.

The tardy bell rang. Allie bit her lower lip. *Poor Max,* she thought.

Before the echo of the bell faded, Max came bounding through the doorway. He hurried to his table and was about to sit down when—

"Mr. McCrane," Miss Hinkle said, adjusting her glasses. "Come to my desk, please."

Max glanced across the room at Allie. She shrugged as if to say, *Sorry, Max!*

"You, too, Miss O'Dell," Miss Hinkle added. "My desk."

Allie's eyes widened in a look of *uh-oh.*

"And Mr. Stubblefield," Miss Hinkle said. "You, too."

"Me?" Grady said. "I didn't do anything!"

"I never said you did," the teacher replied. She beckoned with her index finger. "Up here, please."

Grady, Allie, and Max gathered around Miss Hinkle's desk.

In a lowered voice, the teacher said, "I want to talk to the three of you about Invention Convention. You're the only ones who haven't turned in a written plan for your project."

Max breathed a sigh of relief. He wasn't in trouble after all.

Grady said, "I was going to turn it in, Miss Hinkle, but—"

"I know, Grady," the teacher replied. "In fact, all three of you have a good reason for not handing in your invention plan on time. Mr. McCrane just transferred to our school—he wasn't here when the assignment was given. Mr. Stubblefield's father is in the hospital. And Miss O'Dell, I know your father won't be able to help you because of—" She hesitated.

"Because of the divorce," Allie said with a resigned shrug.

Max glanced at Allie in surprise. She seemed to take her parents' divorce so calmly and casually.

Miss Hinkle shifted in her chair. "Now, for the benefit of Mr. McCrane," she continued, "I'll explain how Invention Convention works. First, you come up with an idea for your invention, write up a plan, and turn it in to me. After I approve your plan, you build your invention. In four weeks, the inventions will be displayed in the school cafeteria. If your project wins the grand prize, it will be entered in the regional contest. If it wins again, it will go to the state contest, and if it wins there, it will be entered in the national contest. The national winner gets a thousand-dollar savings bond and an appearance on *The Late Show with David Letterman.*"

"Cool!" said Allie O'Dell. She wanted to become an actress someday and couldn't wait to be on national TV—then she frowned. "But I don't have an idea for an invention," she said.

Grady shrugged. "Neither do I."

"I have a *great* idea," Max said. "I'm good at inventions."

"Er—yes, Mr. McCrane," Miss Hinkle said, "so I've heard. For example, the machine you demonstrated at Debockel Middle School—"

Max bit his lip. "Oh, you heard about that?"

"Well," Miss Hinkle said, forcing a tight little smile, "let bygones be bygones, I always say. Just check with me before you test any inventions on school property."

"I will," Max promised.

"Good," Miss Hinkle said with a relieved sigh. "Well, since Mr. McCrane already has an idea, why don't the three of you work together?"

Max gulped. "Us . . . on one team?"

Grady grimaced. "Me? Work with *him?*"

Miss Hinkle looked sharply at Grady. "Do you have a better plan, Mr. Stubblefield?"

Grady shook his head, scowling.

"Then it's settled," the teacher said. She took a pencil in hand. "Now, what is your idea, Mr. McCrane?"

Max paused. "It's called Timebender," he said.

"Timebender?" Miss Hinkle asked. "What does it do?"

"It takes you to the past or the future," Max said.

"A time machine!" Allie chirped. "Cool!"

"What a geek!" Grady sneered.

Miss Hinkle shot Grady a scolding look, then turned to Max. "Mr. McCrane," she said, "your invention must fit in one of two categories—Practical Inventions or Wacky Contraptions. Practical Inventions are ideas that actually work. Wacky Contraptions are wild, imaginative ideas for fun. I'm afraid only Practical Inventions are eligible for the grand prize. Wacky Contraptions like your Timebender—"

"But Timebender *is* a Practical Invention," Max insisted. "It *works!*"

Miss Hinkle sighed. "Tell you what—build your Timebender and prove it works, and I'll let you enter it as a Practical Invention."

Max knew his teacher didn't think there was one chance in a zillion that his time machine would work. "Okay," he said. "But it *will* work. And it'll win the grand prize."

It was 3:15 P.M., and the school day was over at last.

The yellow school bus idled and rattled at the curb. Grady

Stubblefield climbed aboard and found a place near the middle of the bus. He slid over by the window, tossing his backpack onto the seat to keep anyone from sitting beside him. As he leaned against the window, his smooth ebony features were reflected in the glass. He shut his eyes tightly.

Grady didn't have many friends at school. Kids avoided him because he acted mean and bossy. They didn't know that the reason he was so tough on the outside was that he was hurting on the inside. It wasn't a physical pain. It was worse, much worse. Grady was going home to an empty house. His mother wouldn't be there—she was at the hospital with his dad. And Grady was afraid of what was going to happen next.

Grady thought about last night when he had visited his dad. It scared him to see his father in that hospital room, so weak and thin, with tubes and machines all around him.

"Does it hurt?" Grady had asked.

"Not much," his father had replied. "I'm doing all right."

But Grady knew his father wasn't all right. Neither the doctors nor Grady's mother would say much, but everyone seemed very grim.

Just a week earlier, as Grady and his mother were at home, cleaning up the dinner dishes, he had asked her, "Why isn't Dad getting better? Why doesn't God answer our prayers?"

"God always answers our prayers," his mother had told him. "But sometimes the answer is 'No.'"

That had troubled Grady. He had always assumed that God would say "Yes" to his prayers. He had assumed his father would get well and would come home from the hospital, and everything would be the way it used to be. But when his mother told him that God's answer might be "No," Grady became scared that his dad might never come home again. Lately, he had begun wondering if God was even listening to his prayers.

Max was the last to board the bus. By the time he got on, almost every seat was taken. He paused at the front, searching the rows of seats. The driver—a large woman in a starched white shirt and black pants—drummed her fingers on the steering wheel. "Sonny," she said, "find a seat so I can get this bus in gear."

Max nodded and walked down the aisle. The bus was noisy with students' chatter. The air was dense and hot. Halfway down the aisle, Max spotted an empty seat. He hurried toward it and was about to sit down—

Then he saw that the seat, which was next to Grady Stubblefield, had a backpack in it. Grady shot Max a threatening glare. Max decided to sit elsewhere.

Max turned and saw Allie across the aisle with a book in her lap. As she read, she pulled a purple scrunchie off her ponytail and her carrot-red hair fell in front of her face.

Absently, she pulled it back to a ponytail and twisted the scrunchie back on. She looked up to see Max. Smiling, she moved her backpack to the floor. "There's a seat right here," she said brightly.

Max settled into the seat, and the bus lurched forward with a diesel cough and a clash of gears. Max shouted over the noise, "What are you reading?"

Allie held up the cover. *"The White Dragon of Zarvane* by J. Farthington Frimby," she said. "It's almost as good as *Blood of the Golden Dragon.* I love books about dragons. What about you?"

Max shook his head. "I'm not into fantasy. I like science fiction."

"Aha!" Allie said. "That's where you got the idea for Timebender."

"Sure," Max said. "The cool thing about science fiction is that it can really happen. Fantasy is just make-believe."

"I don't know," Allie said. "I think fantasy stories are just as possible as science fiction stories. After all, dragons might have been real, once upon a time."

Max laughed.

"I'm serious," Allie said. "Maybe what we call dinosaurs were actually dragons. Maybe dragon legends were based on *real* dragons like Tyrannosaurus rex!"

"Come on!" Max scoffed.

"Well, why not?" Allie said. "Dinosaurs look like dragons, don't they? Maybe a T. rex could breathe fire. Maybe flying pterodactyls came in different colors and their skin was covered with jewels, like in *Rainbow Dragons of the Sky*."

"I know all about dinosaurs," Max said, "and they didn't breathe fire, and they weren't covered with jewels. Dinosaurs were *not* dragons, and that's *that*."

"Well," Allie said, "I wish I could meet one and see for myself."

"Meet what?" asked Max. "A dragon? Or a dinosaur?"

Allie laughed. "Either, or both."

"Well," Max said, "maybe you'll get your wish."

"What do you mean?"

"Timebender," Max said. "We can use it to hunt *real* dinosaurs. And real dragons, too, if they ever existed."

Allie laughed. "You're funny! I just about died when you told Miss Hinkle you were going to build a *real* time machine!"

"I'll let you in on a secret," Max said. "I've already built Timebender. And it *works*."

Allie's eyes flashed. "Look, Max," she said, "a joke is a joke—but time travel is impossible!"

Max's face was serious. "You're wrong, Allie, and I'll prove it. Come home with me after school today and I'll show you."

"Oh, right!" Allie giggled. "You would so-o-o freak out if I said yes! But I can't come today—I've got karate class. How about tomorrow morning? It's Saturday, no school. I can come over at—"

"Nine o'clock?"

"Make it ten," Allie said. "Well, ten-ish. I like to sleep late on Saturdays." She reached into her backpack and pulled out a spiral-bound notebook. "Here," she said, handing the notebook to Max. "Draw me a map so I can find your house."

"Okay." Max took the notebook and began drawing. "My house is right here—past Fell Drive, at the end of Mirabilis Way."

Allie nodded. "Oh, wow! You live near that big, scary-looking haunted house!"

Max chuckled. "That haunted house *is* my house."

Allie winced. "Sorry."

"That's okay. It looks scary outside, but it's fun inside. The rooms go on forever. I'll give you a tour."

"Cool," Allie said. "I love haun—I love big, old houses." She reached over and flipped the notebook to another page. "Now draw another map."

"Why?"

"Just draw."

Max shrugged and drew a second map. Allie ripped the map out of the notebook and folded it a couple of times.

The bus came to a stop with a squeal of tortured brakes. Across the aisle from Max and Allie, Grady got up and slung his backpack over his shoulder.

"Grady, wait!" Allie called. She leaned across Max and handed the folded map to Grady.

Grady looked at it. "What's this?"

"Directions to Max's house," Allie said. "Be there at ten tomorrow morning. We'll work on our project for Invention Convention."

"What are you doing?" Max asked in a horrified whisper.

Grady tossed the map back to Allie. "I don't waste time with *losers.*"

Allie stuffed it back into Grady's hand. Her eyes were stormy. "Listen, Grady Stubblefield," she said in a tone that would curdle milk, "the world is *not* divided into winners and losers! We're all the same—no one's better or worse than anyone else! Max invited us to his house—"

"But I didn't invite—," Max began.

"—so quit acting like a jerk," Allie finished, "and be there at ten!"

Grady's eyes smoldered.

"On or off, sonny!" the driver bellowed. "This bus can't wait all day!"

Frowning, Grady stuffed the map in his shirt pocket.

Max breathed a sigh of relief as Grady walked to the front of the bus and got off. Turning to Allie, Max said, "Why did you invite him to my house? He *hates* me!"

"*What a couple of dorks!*" said a voice from the seat ahead.

Startled, Max and Allie looked up and saw Toby Brubaker's pale eyes peering at them. "Dude! I heard everything you guys said. 'Timebender,' huh? You dorks really think you can build a time machine?"

Max clenched his teeth. He didn't like Toby any more than he liked Grady. "Timebender works," Max said, "and it's going to win."

"Yeah, right," Toby said. "Wait'll you guys see *my* invention. It'll be a hundred times better than some fake time machine!" He turned around, laughing until he snorted through his nose.

"Just ignore him," Allie said.

"Timebender *does* work," Max said. "I'll prove it to you, Allie. I'll prove it to everybody."

Grady stepped off the bus, and the door hissed shut behind him. He paused on the sidewalk, grimacing at the oily cloud of exhaust as the bus rumbled away. Grady had already forgotten about the map in his shirt pocket. He had other things to worry about.

He turned and started for home.

It wasn't far from the bus stop to his house—two blocks up Quincy Avenue, then half a block left on Poplar Way. As Grady walked along, he felt the warmth of the afternoon sun on his arms and face. A few yards to his right, he saw a pair of gray squirrels chasing each other across a lawn and up a tree trunk, chattering *kuk-kuk-kuk* as they ran. It was all perfectly familiar—

Yet, *something* wasn't right.

With every step he took toward home, he felt something gnawing at his insides. Something was wrong. It was a dark feeling, as if a shadow of deep sadness was passing over him. His footsteps slowed—then stopped. He shivered. His heart pounded.

Then, as suddenly as it came, the darkness lifted. Grady sensed a voice say, *Everything's all right now, Grady.* It sounded like his father's voice. It sounded so real that Grady turned and looked behind him—but his father wasn't there.

Not there! he thought with a sudden rush of horror. *Dad? Dad!* In that instant, Grady sensed it was true: His father, his best friend, was no longer in the world.

He felt as if he had been slugged in the stomach. He could hardly breathe, and there was a huge lump of hurt in his chest. Hoping he was wrong, he began to run home.

2

UGLY ORANGE BEETLE

Allie willed her feet to walk clear to the end of Mirabilis Way, right up to the front walk of the strange old house. "It's a bright, sunny Saturday morning," she told herself, "and that's the house where Max lives. Nothing to be scared about!"

Still, this was the notorious McCrane House, the one house in town that trick-or-treaters avoided on Halloween. For years, Allie had heard rumors about this strange old Victorian house—rumors of mysterious disappearances and gruesome discoveries. Of course, Allie didn't put any stock in rumors, but she couldn't help wondering. . . .

The house was more than a hundred years old, and it had been built when there was nothing surrounding it but walnut groves. Over the years, the suburbs had crawled out along Mirabilis Way, so that the old McCrane House now sat at the end of a street lined with suburban split-level homes with sloping front lawns and trees and mailboxes. In this modern neighborhood, the old mansion looked strangely out-of-place with its turrets and towers topped by witches'-hat roofs and groves of ancient walnut trees surrounding it on both sides.

Allie's piano teacher lived a block from the McCrane House, so Allie had often seen it from a distance. To her active imagination, the house had always seemed alive and hostile, a three-story monstrosity with its shoulders hunched against the sky. But now, seen up-close, the old "haunted house" appeared more like an enchanted mansion, a museum full of memories and secrets.

Allie saw that the house was made of intricate shapes and textures: fish-scale shingles, gingerbread trim, hipped roofs, gables, eaves, ornamental iron, balconies, porches, bay windows, and recessed arcades. She climbed up the steps to the porch and stopped in front of the ornate scroll on the door that read:

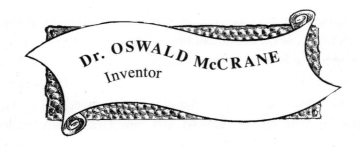

Dr. OSWALD McCRANE
Inventor

Allie pressed the doorbell. Moments later, the door swung open, and there was Max. He was wearing cargo pants and a white Hurley tee shirt. "Hi, Allie," he said. "Come in."

Allie crossed the threshold. "This," she said, looking around the entryway, "is a cool house!"

"That's the east wing down that way," Max said, pointing. "My laboratory's down there, at the end of the hall. That's where I built Timebender."

"You have your own laboratory?" Allie said. "Cool! Let's go see it."

"In a minute," Max said. "First, I want you to meet my dad. His laboratory's at the far end of the west wing."

He led her down a long hallway with many doors, most of them closed and locked. (*Very mysterious!* Allie thought.) "This house goes on forever!" she marveled out loud. "How many rooms are there?"

"I don't know," Max said. "I asked my dad once, and even he doesn't know. I've explored every floor of this house, from top to bottom. Every once in a while, I find a room I've never seen before. Sometimes, when I go back and look for the room, I can't find it. My dad says he thinks some of the rooms in this house exist in a different dimension."

Allie laughed. "He's kidding—right?"

Max shrugged. "I don't know. I don't think so."

Rooms that appeared and disappeared? Rooms that existed in different dimensions? Allie remembered those rumors about strange disappearances—and she suppressed a shudder.

"Well, here we are, my dad's laboratory," Max said, stopping before a closed door at the end of the hall. He knocked on the door. "I think you'll like my dad."

The door swung open on creaking hinges. A man stepped forward who looked like an older version of Max. He had an unruly thatch of hair the same brown color as Max's. His brown eyes were magnified behind large, round glasses like Max's.

"Dad, this is Allie," said Max.

"Nice to meet you, Sally," said Dr. McCrane.

"It's Allie, Dad," Max said—but he said it quickly so that "It's" and "Allie" scrunched together and sounded like "It's Sally."

"I heard you the first time," Dr. McCrane said, giving his son a befuddled look.

"But Dad—," Max said as they stepped into the lab.

"Never mind," Allie whispered, staring in wonder at the McCrane laboratory. "This place looks like Dr. Frankenstein's basement!"

It did, indeed. Dr. McCrane's lab was a huge chamber filled with electrical equipment that buzzed and hummed, flashed and flickered, sparked and glowed. Some machines had big glass tubes that pulsed with blue, red, or purple light. Others had lights that pinwheeled, flickered, vibrated, sparked, or popped in a cascade of colors. Each burst of brilliant light sent weird shadows jitterbugging across the room.

"What is all this stuff?" Allie asked as multicolored lights danced in her wide, astonished eyes. "What does it all do?"

"That," Dr. McCrane said, pointing to a monstrous machine, "is a Wimshurst electrostatic influence generator. It can generate a single spark of a hundred thousand volts. Uh, don't touch that, Sally."

"Wouldn't think of it," Allie said, backing away.

"And that," Dr. McCrane said, "is an Oudin Oscillator. We use it to produce high-potential antinodes."

"I see," Allie said, completely clueless.

"And over here we have our Tesla transformer, our molecular sieve, our high-energy omegatron, our polari-scope, our mass spectrometer, our Toepler pump, our voltaic pile, and our induction coils. And over against that wall we have our Klystrons, magnetrons, thyratrons, and Mrs. McCrane. Oh, hello, dear. Where did you come from?"

Mrs. McCrane was a thin woman with brown hair, a lined face, and worried-looking eyes. With her right hand, she held down a lever on a machine with flashing blue lights. She flashed a quick smile in Allie's direction. "Nice to meet you, Sally," she said, then turned to her husband. "Don't you remember, Oswald? You asked me to come in here and hold down this phase thingy—"

"Ah, yes," Dr. McCrane said, "the phase frequency lever."

"Can I let go now?" asked Mrs. McCrane.

"Of course, dear," Dr. McCrane said. "The phase tests were finished thirty minutes ago."

"Oh, Oswald!" she snorted, releasing the lever. "You mean I've been sitting here for the past half-hour, holding down this silly lever for no reason at all?"

"I—I'm sorry, dear. I guess I forgot."

"You forgot!" Mrs. McCrane threw her hands up. "Oswald, I declare, you are the most absent-minded man! Whatever happened to that memory course I bought you?"

"Memory course, dear?" Dr. McCrane blinked behind his thick-lensed glasses. "I don't remember any—"

"The Anne M. Nesia Retrain-Your-Brain Max-O-Memory Course! Big book, six cassettes—I gave it to you last Christmas."

"Oh, that!" Dr. McCrane scratched his head. "I'm planning to try it out—as soon as I remember where I put it."

"Well," Max said, "you're all busy, so we'll just be moving along."

"Max is going to show me his time machine," Allie said.

"Oh, yes! Timewinder!" Dr. McCrane exclaimed. "Marvelous idea. Max has a wonderful imagination."

"It's Time*bender*, Dad," Max said.

Dr. McCrane blinked. "Isn't that what I said?"

"It's been nice meeting you both," Allie said.

Max and Allie left the laboratory and closed the door

behind them. "Your dad says you have 'a wonderful imagination,'" Allie said. "Sounds like he doesn't believe Timebender works."

"He hasn't seen it in operation," Max said. "But you will."

"Okay, Max," Allie said, "lead me to this time machine of yours."

"Right this way," Max said.

He led Allie down the hallway. As they reached the entryway, the doorbell chimed. Peering through the stained glass of the door, they saw someone on the front porch.

"Oh, no!" Max groaned. "It's *him!* I'm not opening that door!"

"Then I will," Allie said.

"No! Wait!" But Max wasn't fast enough to stop Allie. She pulled the door open and—

"Grady!" Allie said cheerfully. "I didn't think you would come!"

Grady stood unsmiling with his hands thrust in his pockets. "Okay, I'm here. Don't make a big deal about it." He stepped into the entry hall and looked all around. "No offense, McCrane, but your house is really weird."

"Yeah," Max said. "No offense. So why did you come? I thought you had better things to do than hang out with *losers.*"

Grady eyed Max without expression. "My dad died yesterday," he said.

Allie gasped. "Oh, Grady!" She reached out to him.

Grady pulled back. "Look," he snapped, "I don't want your pity!"

Max knew, especially under the circumstances, he should try to be nice to the guy—but Max still remembered the way Grady had yelled and shoved his fist in Max's face just the day before. "So what *do* you want?" said Max.

Grady shrugged. "Maybe I just want to get my mind off things," he answered sullenly.

It was clear to Max that Grady had some important reason for coming—he hadn't just come to "get his mind off things." When a guy's dad has just died, he doesn't leave home to go work on a science project. At a time like that, a guy would naturally want to be with his family. So why had Grady come over? It was a mystery, and Max was determined to figure it out.

"Doesn't your mom need you at home?" Allie asked.

Grady shook his head. "She's out making funeral arrangements. My aunt's staying at the house. I locked my bedroom door, climbed out the window—and my aunt thinks I'm still in my room." He turned to Max. "So, McCrane, are you going to show me this geeky invention of yours or not?"

"Sure," Max said. "Follow me."

Max pushed the door of his laboratory open and stepped aside for Allie and Grady to enter. "Ladies and doubters first," he said. Allie entered, stopped, and stared. Then Grady did the same.

"Max," Allie said while blinking, "you have a *car* in your house."

And he did! He had many other things in his laboratory as well: electrical devices—though none were as big and dangerous-looking as his dad's Wimshurst electrostatic influence generator—and a complete chemistry lab, equipped with beakers, retorts, measuring cylinders, test tubes, racks, desiccators, a Bunsen burner, and a large case stocked with rows of powders and liquid chemicals in bottles. All the chemicals left a sour, acidy tang in the air.

But, of course, the one thing that dominated the room was the dented old Volkswagen Beetle. Its windshield was cracked. The rear deck lid was raised, showing an empty hole where the motor should have been. Stuffing protruded from the seat covers. And then there was the color—

"It's so *orange!*" Allie said, making a face.

She was right. The car was a perfectly nauseating shade of bright orange—faded in some places, rusted through in others, but all in all, it was about as orange as orange could be.

"It's really old, too," said Max. "It's a '64—one of the original VW Beetles, with the trunk in front and the motor in back. My dad says it's just like the one he drove when he was in college."

"McCrane," Grady said, "that's the ugliest car I've ever seen."

"Max," Allie said, "why do you have a car in your house?"

"That's not just a car," Max said proudly. "That's *it*."

"That's *what?*" Allie asked.

"Our time machine. That ugly orange Beetle is going to win the grand prize at Invention Convention. Grady, Allie—meet Timebender."

Grady and Allie walked all the way around the car.

"How did you get it in your house?" Allie asked.

"In pieces," Max said. "My dad and I bought it at a junkyard for thirty bucks. We towed it home, took it apart, and carried the pieces in here. We put it together right where you see it."

"Why didn't you just work on it outside?" Allie asked.

"My mom asked the same question. I guess my dad and I just didn't think of that."

Grady scratched his head. "Your dad knows you're building a time machine—and he's okay with that?"

Max shrugged. "Why not? He doesn't think it'll work."

"Neither do I," Grady said sourly. "I think the whole idea is stupid."

"Then why are you here?" Max asked.

Grady was quiet as he weighed whether or not to tell Max and Allie the truth. Finally, he said, "I'm here because of my dad."

Allie looked baffled. "I don't get it."

Grady leaned against the Beetle's rear fender. "I was awake all last night," he said softly, "just thinking about how I was never going to see my dad again. That was the worst night of my life. You could cut off my arms and legs, and it wouldn't hurt as bad as I hurt last night. But around dawn it hit me: 'What about McCrane's time machine?'"

"I still don't get it," Allie said.

"Look," answered Grady, "I'm not saying I believe in time travel, but just on the crazy chance that McCrane is on to something, I decided to check it out. I mean, just think about the possibilities. Let's say we really can hop in this car and go back in time a year or two—"

"Ohmygosh! I get it. If Timebender works, you'd get to see your dad again! You could go back in time and visit him whenever you want! It would be almost like he never died!"

"I wouldn't just *visit* my dad," Grady said. "I'd go back to a time before he got sick and tell him to see a doctor before it's too late. Don't you get it? If I can go back in time, I can *save my dad's life!*" He paused and glared at Max. "That is, if this whole Timebender thing isn't just a big hoax."

"It's not a hoax," said Max. "I said Timebender works and it does."

"Fine," Grady said. "Let's see some proof."

"Okay," Max said defensively. "You want proof? I'll give you proof."

3

THIS ISN'T SCIENCE FICTION

Toby Brubaker crouched in the shadows of the ancient walnut grove. His pale green eyes peered up through the tree branches, checking out the dark, forbidding towers of the old McCrane House. Toby's body tensed. He had heard many tales about the McCrane mansion—tales of ghosts and mysterious disappearances, not to mention tales of the nutty inventor and the millions he supposedly had stashed in the walls of the weird old house. Toby believed every one of those rumors. Though tales of hidden treasure intrigued him, the rumors of hauntings sent a creepy sensation up his spine.

He had been hiding and spying when Allie went in. That was shocking enough—but then Grady walked up to the front door, rang the doorbell, and walked right inside the haunted house! Were they crazy?

Well, serves 'em right, Toby thought. *Let 'em disappear and never be heard from again—and McCrane, too! Him and his dorky time machine! Thinks he can show me up with some fake invention! I'll show him. I'll show all of them!*

Hiding near the weird old McCrane House, Toby felt scared. He hated being afraid—but he liked being mad. When he was mad, he looked big, he talked tough, he felt important. When he was full of anger, he had no room inside for fear. So as he hid among the trees, he tried to talk himself into being really mad.

Checking the street to make sure no one was watching, Toby stepped out of the shadows and crept across the lawn toward the old house.

Max opened the door of the Volkswagen, slid in behind the steering wheel, and pulled a computer keyboard out from between the bucket seats. A cable snaked from the back of the keyboard to the underside of the dashboard. Setting the keyboard across his lap, Max reached over and popped open the glove box. Inside were a toggle switch and a battery rack holding four Energizer batteries, size D.

Grady stood by the open door of the car, watching Max work. "This thing runs on flashlight batteries?"

"Sure," said Max. He flipped the power switch. A little

yellow light came on in the corner of the keyboard. "Time travel doesn't take a lot of power. Four flashlight batteries are all you need."

Allie pointed to a pair of pocket calculators fastened to the dashboard with strips of gray duct tape. "What are those for?" she asked.

"I rewired those calculators to display the time coordinates," Max said. "Watch." He tapped on the keypad. A series of red characters lit up one of the calculator displays. A few more taps, and the second calculator displayed a series of numbers. "The one on the left shows your target date—how far back in time you want to go. The one on the right displays the return time. You can set Timebender to stay in the past for a set amount of time, then automatically return to the present. I use that for unmanned tests, like the one we're about to do."

Allie wrinkled her nose. "Max, the stench of those chemicals is really getting to me. Okay if I open a window?"

"Go ahead," Max said, pointing to a large window.

Outside, Toby peered into the house. He couldn't believe what he saw. There was a *car* in that room—a beat-up old Volkswagen Beetle. And—

Uh-oh!—

Toby ducked, his heart hammering. Allie was walking toward the window! *What if she saw me?* he thought. *What if those dorks catch me?*

He pressed himself against the wall and waited. Seconds later, he heard Allie raise the window, *whump!* He waited to hear Allie's voice accusing him of spying.

Finally, Toby looked. There was no one at the window.

Gathering his nerve, he raised himself up to peer over the window sill. Allie had gone back to the car and was watching Max.

She didn't see me! Toby thought. *And this is perfect! Dude! I can hear everything those dorks are saying!*

"How does it work, Max?" Allie asked, leaning on the open car door.

"The science is pretty simple," Max said, sitting in the driver's seat. "See these?" He pointed inside the car. Grady and Allie could see bundles of clear plastic filaments that snaked over the doorframe of the car, down along the chassis, and around all the windows. They were held in place by strips of duct tape. "Those are optical fibers," Max said. "They're like wires, only instead of carrying electricity, they carry light. Those fibers are wrapped around the inside of the car in the shape of a Klein bottle."

"A *what* bottle?" Allie asked.

"A Klein bottle," Max said, "named after Felix Klein, a mathematician. A Klein bottle isn't like a regular glass bottle that holds water. It's a weird kind of four-dimensional bottle—its inside is also its outside."

Grady scowled. "Sounds like a lot of double-talk."

"Look," Max said, "I'm explaining it the best I can. If you don't believe me, there's my computer. You can look up Klein bottles on the Internet."

"Whatever," Grady said. "Just get on with it."

"I will—if you'll quit interrupting," Max said. "I experimented with Klein bottle geometry. I found that if you cause light to flow in the shape of a Klein bottle, you actually force the light to pass through the fourth dimension. The fourth dimension, of course, is *time*. When light passes through the fourth dimension, the photons behave like chronons."

"What are chronons?" Allie asked.

"Time particles," Max said. "The chronons circulate around the Volkswagen chassis and time becomes bent—"

"So Timebender actually does *bend* time?" Allie asked.

"Of course," Max said proudly.

"Look, McCrane," Grady said, "the smartest scientists in the world can't figure out how to build a time machine. But you're asking us to believe that some middle-school kid has it all figured out?"

"I really don't care what you believe," Max said defensively. "I figure the reason the smartest scientists never discovered the Timebender principle is that it's so *simple*."

He shrugged. "So, you guys ready for a demonstration?"

Allie nodded enthusiastically.

Grady said, "Go ahead. Show me."

"Stand back," Max said, "and prepare to be amazed. The moment I hit ENTER, we have ten seconds." Max checked his wristwatch—then pressed ENTER. He set the keyboard aside, jumped out of the car, and slammed the door.

Max, Grady, and Allie retreated to the edge of the room. "Don't take your eyes off it!" Max said. "Six seconds . . . five . . . four . . ."

Peering over the window sill, Toby saw the ugly orange VW Beetle, and beyond it, Max, Allie, and Grady, huddled by the wall. Max was counting down: "Three . . . two . . ."

What does McCrane think he's doing? Toby wondered.

"One!" yelled Max.

The ugly orange Beetle was there.

And then it wasn't. It had disappeared.

There was a loud *whoosh!*—the sound of air rushing to fill a vacuum.

Toby yelped in surprise. He couldn't help himself. He had never seen a car *disappear* before. His startled yelp was so loud that Max, Allie, and Grady certainly should have heard him, except for one thing—they were making too much noise themselves.

Allie screamed.

Grady yelled.

Max laughed.

The car was gone. Vanished. *Poof!* Where it had stood mere seconds before there was now only empty floor—and a shiny black splotch of gooey black oil.

Grady slowly walked over to the place where Timebender had been. He reached his hand out as if to convince himself that his eyes weren't deceiving him.

"Where did it go, Max?" Allie asked.

"I set it to go one year into the past," Max said. "At least, I'm pretty sure I did."

Grady glanced up. "*Pretty* sure?"

Max shrugged. "I'm not certain I have all the math figured out. I won't know for sure until I actually ride in it and see where it goes." He checked his watch. "Grady," he yelled, "MOVE BACK!"

Grady jumped backward just as . . . *Poof!* . . . Timebender returned. And right where Grady had been standing.

Grady turned to Max. "Okay, McCrane, you convinced me. Timebender works—just like you said it would. Let's go back two years—that should be enough time to warn my dad and save his life."

Max bit his lower lip. "I don't think that's such a good idea," he said.

"Max!" Allie said, her eyes full of shock.

"What do you mean, McCrane?" Grady demanded.

"Look, Grady," Max said, "I *want* to help you, but—"

Grady took a step toward Max. "But what?"

"It's one thing to go back in time to *observe* history," Max said, "but you want to go back to *change* history. Changing the past could create a time paradox."

"Paradox?" Allie asked. "What's a paradox?"

"A paradox is an idea that logically violates itself," Max said. "Grady, if you go back in time and warn your dad, he'll go to the doctor and get well, right? And you'll come back to your own time, and when you get here, your father will be alive, right? But you'll also know that in your original time-line, your dad *really did* die—and that's a paradox. You'll know that something that never happened actually did happen, only you made it *un*happen. Don't you see, Grady? If you do this, you'll be tying the fourth dimension up in knots!"

Grady scowled. "I don't care about the fourth dimension. I just want to see my dad again."

"Trust me, Grady," Max said. "I've read lots of science fiction. Time paradoxes never turn out well."

Allie grabbed Max by the arm and spun him around. "Max McCrane!" she said, her face red with fury. "This isn't science fiction! This is real life! A paradox thingy is just a guess—you don't really know if it's true or not. But Grady's father *died*—and that's *reality*. If you can change that, then you have to do it!"

Max pulled away from her. "Come on, Allie! I thought *you* would understand."

"All I understand," Allie said coldly, "is that you won't lift a finger to help a friend."

Max thumbed in Grady's direction. "Him? A *friend?*"

"Okay," Allie said, "Grady may not exactly be your friend—but you're acting like a total jerk! And for what? Some silly theory about paradoxes and tying knots in the fourth dimension and—"

"It's not silly," Max said defensively, "and you're not being fair!"

Allie folded her arms. "Are you going to help him or not?"

Max frowned—then he threw up his hands. "Okay, you win."

"Woohoo!" Allie cheered.

"But," Max said, "if something terrible happens—like if the whole universe blows up because of a time paradox— just remember, I warned you."

"Fine, Max," Allie said. "If the universe explodes, we'll tell everybody it wasn't your fault. Now, what do we need to take with us? Should we take food or something?"

Max shook his head. "We won't be gone that long," he said. "But I'd better check the batteries."

He got in the car, reached into the glove box, and took the four Energizers out of the battery rack. One by one, he pressed the tester dots on the batteries.

"I was afraid of that," he said. "They all test low. I'm lucky Timebender had enough power to make the last jump to the past and back." He climbed out of the car, tossed the old batteries in a wastebasket, and replaced them with a fresh set of copper-top Duracells.

"Are we ready?" Grady asked.

"One more thing," Max said. "We're going to be the first time travelers in history, so we need to record our observations." He snapped his fingers. "I know just the thing!" He spun on his heels and headed for the door.

"Where are you going?" Allie asked.

"To get my dad's camcorder," Max replied. "It's in the hall closet."

"Wait for me!" Grady called, hurrying after Max.

Allie looked around the lab, then dashed after them, shouting, "Hey, guys! Don't leave me here alone!"

Toby peered through the open window. He saw the orange Volkswagen. Max, Allie, and Grady were gone. *I might not get another chance*, he thought.

His heart thumping like a hammer, Toby jumped to his feet and scrambled over the window sill, tumbling head-first into the room. He dashed over to the VW. *A real time machine!* he thought bitterly. *My project won't stand a chance against this thing! No fair! Well, I'll fix McCrane and his stupid Timebender!*

Toby knew exactly how to "fix" Timebender. He had seen Max change the batteries, and he saw where Max threw away the old ones. Working quickly, he retrieved the old Energizer batteries from the wastebasket and swapped them for the new Duracells. *The next trip this thing makes,* Toby thought as he closed the car door, *will be a one-way trip to nowhere. Timebender won't be winning any prizes at Invention Convention, if it runs out of power and gets stuck in the past!*

Voices were coming from the hallway.

Toby froze. He checked the window. Too far away. He looked all around Max's laboratory. No place to hide. He looked at Timebender—

And saw the only hiding place around.

The old Volkswagen Beetles that were made in the 1960s had the motor in the back and a big empty trunk in front. In his panic, Toby opened the hood and climbed inside. The rusty hinges creaked as he pulled the hood down over himself. What Toby didn't know was that there's no handle on the inside of the hood. Once he got inside, he was trapped!

"What was that noise?" Allie called. She was the first to dash back into Max's laboratory. Max and Grady were close behind.

"I heard it, too," Grady said. "Like a car door slamming!"

They rushed to the Volkswagen and checked it over— but everything looked exactly as they had left it.

"That's weird," Max said, cradling the camcorder in his arm. "But this clunky old car is always making noises." He shrugged. "Well, guys, it's time to saddle up and ride the fourth dimension!"

Grady climbed into the back, and Max and Allie sat in front. Max handed the camcorder to Allie, then put the computer keyboard on his lap. "Allie," he said, "would you turn on the power?"

"Okay," she said. When she opened the glove box, the old spent Energizer batteries were sitting there in plain sight—but nobody noticed. Allie toggled the power switch, and the little yellow light came on in the corner of the keyboard. It was weak and dim, but nobody noticed that, either.

Max tapped on the keypad. "By my calculations," he said, "I'm setting Timebender to go back two years." The time coordinates lit up on the calculator displays. "Ten," Max said. "Nine . . . eight . . . seven . . . six . . ."

Five seconds later, Timebender and its passengers vanished.

Moments later, there was a sound of approaching footsteps in the hallway outside Max's laboratory. "I hope you kids are hungry," Mrs. McCrane called. She walked into the room with a tray in her hands. "I brought some milk and cookies for—"

She stopped and stared.

The ugly orange Volkswagen—that horrid old car that Max called "Timebender"—was simply *gone*.

But that was impossible. She had seen it there a short time earlier. And it wouldn't fit through the door.

Suddenly, the tray fell to the floor. Cookies flew. Glasses crashed. Milk splashed everywhere.

Mrs. McCrane ran screaming down the hall.

4

WHEN ARE WE?

They all felt it—a wild lurching sensation in their innards.

"Ooh!" Allie cried. "I think I left my stomach behind—in the future!"

"Do you guys feel dizzy?" Grady asked.

"Yeah," Max said, "like the whole world just flipped over!"

"Look!" Allie pointed beyond the windshield. Max looked. They weren't in the laboratory anymore.

"Uh-oh," he said. "This is wrong, guys. This is *way* wrong. If we only went back two years, we should still be in my house—but the house is completely gone. Something went wrong, and I need to figure it out. Let's go look around."

They scrambled out of the car and checked their surroundings. The Volkswagen sat atop a grassy hill in a sunlit clearing, surrounded by what looked to be a tropical rain forest. The air was hot and steamy. In the distance, jagged purple mountains rose steeply against the sky. Behind the car, the hill sloped down to a swampy, fern-lined stream where muddy brown water flowed around moss-covered rocks.

"McCrane," Grady said, "if the car starts rolling backward, it'll go right into that swamp. You'd better set the parking brake."

"Can't. The parking brake is busted," Max said. He turned and walked toward the edge of the clearing, where plants grew large, lush, and strange.

He waved to Allie. "Hey, bring the camcorder over here!"

"Coming," she said.

He pointed to a treelike plant that branched at the top into a pompom of long green leaves. "Get a shot of this," Max said, fascinated by the plant.

"What is it?" Allie asked as she taped.

"It's called a cycad. These plants are extinct in our own time."

Allie pressed the PAUSE button and lowered the camcorder. "Did you say 'extinct in our own time'?"

Max turned and stared at Allie. In unison, they cried, "UH-OH!"

"Hey!" Grady yelled as he pointed to the sky. "Look at that!"

Max looked and saw a creature flying through the air—

but it didn't look like a bird. It was hard to judge its size from a distance, but it looked *big*. From beak to claw, its body was about as long as a man is tall. The spread of its wings was huge—at least four or five times as broad as a man is tall. The creature soared over the treetops with its leathery wings outstretched.

Allie was frozen in place. Max grabbed the camcorder from her hands, pointed it, and pressed RECORD, zooming in as he taped. Through the viewfinder, he got a good look at the creature's long, narrow head, the leathery wings, the featherless body, the long claws protruding from the middle of the wings—

And he *knew*.

"What *is* that?" Grady asked nervously.

"It's a pteranodon," Max said, lowering the camcorder.

Allie's eyes were wide as she stared at the creature. She was mentally measuring the long jaw, wondering if it had an appetite for five-foot-two redheads from the twenty-first century. The creature disappeared behind some trees. "Wh-What kind of bird is a pteranodon?" she asked in a shaky voice.

"Not a bird," Max said. "A flying reptile. Guys, we kind of overshot."

"Overshot?" Grady asked.

"Where are—," Allie started, then paused. "Maybe I should say—*when* are we?"

"Based on when cycads and pteranodons lived," Max

said, "I'd say we're somewhere in the Cretaceous Period—at least eighty million years in the past."

Allie gasped in shock and her freckled face went pale.

Grady's eyes widened and his mouth opened and closed—but no words came out. Finally, he blurted, "McCrane, you were supposed to take us back *two* years—not eighty million! What kind of stupid—"

Max shrugged. "I guess I miscalculated."

"You *guess!*" Grady yelled, gesturing wildly. "You *guess?*"

"Easy, Grady," Allie said. "Yelling at each other won't solve anything."

"If you'll remember," Max said, "I didn't even want to—"

Whump-whump-whump!

All three of them jumped at the sudden pounding noise from the Volkswagen.

"What was *that?*" Allie asked, an edge of panic in her voice.

The sound came again: *Whump-whump-whump!* Then they heard a muffled voice: "Hey, you dorks! I'm suffocating in here!" As they stared at the ugly orange car, it began to rock from side to side, as if someone were inside, struggling to get out.

Allie's eyes went wide with recognition. "That sounds like Toby Brubaker!"

Max ran toward the car. "Toby? Don't move! Stop rocking the car!"

But the car kept rocking. "Let me out of here!" Toby yelled.

"Ohmygosh!" Allie said. "Max, it's starting to roll!"

The car was rolling backward, down the hill toward the swampy stream—and it was picking up speed. Max, Allie, and Grady chased after the runaway Volkswagen, but halted when they realized they couldn't stop it.

"Dude! Get me out of here!" came Toby's muffled cry.

The Beetle bounced down the hill and hit the swamp with a mighty, muddy splash. The hood popped up—and there, huddled in a trembling ball, was Toby. Max and Grady dashed down the hill, followed closely by Allie. Each boy grasped one of Toby's arms. "Let go of me! Let go of me!" he yelled. Max and Grady pulled Toby out of the car and dumped him—not too gently—on the ground.

Toby jumped to his feet, red-faced and furious. "What are you guys trying to do—kill me?" He pointed to the tire tracks in the grass, leading from the top of the hill all the way to the bottom. "You guys *pushed* me down that hill! You—" Toby's mouth snapped shut and his eyes popped wide open. "Hey . . . McCrane . . . ," he said slowly, "where did your house go?"

"It's about eighty million years in the future," Allie said.

Toby looked back at Allie with a blank expression. "Eighty . . . million . . . years?"

"Now, what are *you* doing here?" Allie asked.

"It's obvious why he's here," Max said. "He sneaked into my lab. He was trying to wreck Timebender."

"That's the noise we heard—Brubaker slamming the hood!" Grady said.

"Is that right, Toby?" Allie asked. "Were you trying to wreck Max's time machine?"

Caught and not sure what to say or do, Toby glared sullenly. "I don't have to explain anything to you guys!" he snapped.

Max was about to reply, but a shout from Allie cut him off. "Oh, no! Look at that!" She pointed to the rear end of the car, submerged in foul brown water to the top of its hubcaps. "We'll never get Timebender out of that mud."

Max bent down for a closer look. "No problem," he said. "We can timebend out of here."

There was a sudden screeching from the sky. All four looked up and saw that the pteranodon was back—and it had brought a friend. The two pteranodons circled like giant hawks in the sky.

"Max, what do pteranodons eat?" Allie asked.

"Meat," Max said.

"I think we should get out of here—before we all end up as Dinosaur Chow," she said.

"Yeah," Max said. "Let's go home. Everybody, get back in the car."

"Too late!" Grady hollered, pointing.

Max looked where Grady pointed, and he saw *dinosaurs*. They weren't large, as dinosaurs go—only about four feet high. They emerged from among the plants and trees that surrounded the clearing, and they approached with eyes that were large, red, and reptilian.

They had short, stubby forelimbs, and they walked on two legs. They were long—about seven feet from snout to tail. Their necks were stretched straight out in front of them and their tails pointed straight behind them. Their skin was mottled green and yellow, and a row of stubby, hornlike knobs crowned the rear of their heads.

More than twenty of them surrounded the four young time travelers.

"Max," Allie said, her voice rising to a mousy squeak, "I don't know much about dinosaurs, but I recognize those! They're Velociraptors!"

"Velociraptors!" yelled Grady and Toby together. Without waiting for Max and Allie, they pulled the driver's door open and dived into the car.

"Wait for me!" Allie cried, diving in behind them. "Max," she called, "get in here!"

Max looked around at the circle of dinosaurs—

And he *laughed!*

The green-and-yellow dinosaurs jumped back, startled by Max's laughter. They eyed him with curiosity, then crept a step closer. Max slowly advanced toward the nearest one and gently put out his hand. The dinosaur sniffed it.

"Max!" Allie called from the car. "What are you doing?"

Max rubbed the dinosaur's head. It closed its eyes and nuzzled Max's hand. "Come on out, you wusses!" Max said. "These aren't Velociraptors." A purple-pink tongue slithered out of the dinosaur's mouth and licked Max's face, leaving a shiny glob of slobber on his cheek. Max laughed. "This guy is a Stegoceras—a plant-eater from the Cretaceous era. It won't bite. Look, it likes me!"

Allie opened the car door and leaned out. "Are you sure? How do you know it's not a Velociraptor?"

"For one thing, I'm still alive," Max said, grinning. "For another, Velociraptors have a six-inch killing claw on their big toes. Come on out—it's safe. Look, they're just eating fruit!"

They were, indeed. Up the hill a few yards, several Stegocerases were gathered around a large ginkgo tree with broad, fan-shaped leaves and long, snakelike branches. Dozens and dozens of wrinkly ginkgo fruit had fallen onto the ground around the foot of the tree. The Stegocerases ignored the fruit still on the tree, preferring the soft, overripe fruit on the ground. The dinosaurs picked up the plum-sized treats with their clawed, five-fingered hands, gnawed at it with their serrated teeth, then spit the large seeds out on the ground.

As the creatures ate, Max pointed the camcorder at them, capturing them on videotape. Allie left the car and came up behind him. "Go ahead," Max said. "Pet them. They're gentle. I'll take a video of you with the Stegocerases."

Hesitantly, Allie reached out toward one of the creatures. It eyed her warily with one of its huge red eyes. She placed her hand on its snout, and the Stegoceras flinched—but allowed her to touch it.

"There," Max said. "What did I tell you?"

Allie giggled and petted the gentle beast—then she wrinkled her nose. "What's that smell?" she asked. "Eeeww! It's like old gym socks! Is that what a dinosaur smells like?"

Max bent down, picked up one of the fallen ginkgo fruit, sniffed it—then recoiled. "Ooh! It's not the dinosaur!" he said, grimacing. "It's these ginkgo fruit. See?" He held it out for her to sniff.

Allie backed away. "Ginkgo? That stuff should be called 'stinko'!"

Grady and Toby joined Max and Allie by the ginkgo tree. Allie picked up a few of the fallen fruit from the ground and hand-fed the dinosaurs. She squealed—half in fright, half in delight—the first time a purple-pink tongue slithered over those scaly green lips and snatched the fruit from her hand, leaving a puddle of dino-saliva in her upturned palm. Allie's squeal startled the gentle beast at first, but it soon returned to be fed again.

Grady watched Allie feed the dinosaurs, then tried it himself. He laughed when the Stegoceras scarfed down a wrinkly ginkgo fruit from his hand. It made Allie feel good to see a smile on Grady's face.

Toby refused to go near the dinosaurs. He just stood with his hands thrust in his pockets, complaining about the smell. Max captured it all on videotape—Allie's squeals, Grady's smiles, Toby's complaints, and the Stegocerases' slobbery eating habits. After a while, the dinosaurs had eaten all the ginkgo fruit from the ground, leaving the grass littered with drool-covered ginkgo pits. The creatures moved on to a stand of cycads and gnawed on the long, emerald green leaves.

"I'm hungry," Toby whined. "Did any of you dorks think to bring anything to eat?"

"The only thing to eat around here," Allie said, "is fruit that smells like stinky socks. If you want to eat it, that's up to you."

"Dude! I want to go home," Toby said.

"If you'll recall," Max said, "you came along on your own. Anyway, we'll be leaving soon."

"How soon?" Toby asked.

"Soon," Max said.

"I want to know when we'll be home!"

"In about eighty million years," Allie said. "Now, quit being a pest."

Toby opened his mouth, then closed it.

Max and Allie walked along with the Stegocerases, petting them as they munched on cycad leaves. Allie glanced back over her shoulder. Grady was walking down the hill toward the car and the muddy stream. His shoulders were hunched, his hands were in his pockets, and he seemed completely friendless and alone. "I feel sorry for Grady," Allie said.

"I never thought I would," Max said, "but I guess I feel kind of sorry for him, too. It must be awful, losing your dad. I don't know what I'd do if anything happened to my mom or dad."

A cooling breeze wafted through the clearing, stirring the moist, heavy air. The herd of Stegocerases raised their heads and sniffed the breeze.

"Oh, that breeze feels good!" Allie said.

"Yeah," Max said. "Are you glad you came?"

"Are you kidding?" Allie said with a broad grin. "How many people from the twenty-first century ever get this close to a real dinosaur?"

"Yeah, you got your wish, didn't you? Just like I said you would."

"My wish? What wish?"

"On the bus," Max said. "You wished you could meet a dragon or a dinosaur."

"Oh, yeah," Allie said. "And you said, 'Maybe you'll get your wish.' And you were right—although I still haven't seen a dragon yet."

"Who knows? Maybe you'll get to, before we get home."

Allie laughed. "Maybe I will. But I'll settle for just getting home to my mom and . . ." Allie looked away.

There was a long pause before Max said, "Does the divorce really not bother you?"

Allie was smiling, but her smile seemed fragile, as if it could crumble at any moment. Her voice was shaky and her eyes were shiny and moist. "It's no big deal."

"It would be a big deal to me," Max said.

Allie shrugged. "I'll see my dad every other weekend. Sometimes less. We won't be together enough to work on an invention project." A tear glistened at the corner of her eye, but she dabbed at it before it could fall. "In a way, though, that's probably not such a bad thing."

"What do you mean?" asked Max.

"My dad's invention ideas were totally lame," she said. "You know what he wanted us to build? He called it a Personal Shade Machine. Really dumb. You take a hula-hoop, place aluminum foil across the middle to block out the sun, tie a bunch of helium balloons around it to hold it up in the air, then anchor it to your belt with four pieces of string to keep it hovering over you. I would have felt like a total dweeb modeling it."

Max shrugged. "You're right. It does sound stupid."

Allie was silent for several seconds. A tear rolled down her cheek, and this time she didn't try to hide it. "Max," she said, "I'd give anything if my dad and I could have built that stupid machine."

A few moments passed. Max felt awkward, wondering if he should say something else or—

Crash! Splash!

"What was that?" Allie asked.

"Hey! Aaaagh!"

"It came from down the hill, by the stream!" Max said.

"It's Grady!" Allie said. "He's in trouble!"

"Come on!" Max yelled. They rushed past Toby and

ran down the hill. Halfway to the bottom, they stopped. At first they didn't see Grady anywhere—then they spotted him, hiding behind a tree on the far bank. He had waded across the stream, and he was soaked. And the reason he crossed the stream was standing next to the Volkswagen: a four-ton dinosaur.

Apparently, the big, plodding dinosaur had come crashing through a stand of nearby palms and ficus. It had surprised Grady and sent him scurrying across the muddy stream.

"Max, what is that thing?" Allie asked.

"An ankylosaur," Max said, his eyes filled with wonder.

The ankylosaur was about five feet high, eight feet wide, and twenty-five feet from its reptilian head to its clublike tail. It looked a lot like a truck-sized armadillo—only *this* overgrown armadillo had a leathery orange hide. In fact, the ankylosaur was roughly the same shape and the same shade of orange as the VW Beetle. The orange dinosaur began to nuzzle the orange Volkswagen.

"I think that dinosaur has a crush on Timebender," Max said.

"This is no time for jokes!" Allie nearly shrieked.

"I'm not joking," Max said.

"Hey, McCrane," Grady called from across the stream, "does that thing eat meat?"

Max raised the camcorder and zoomed in on the ankylosaur. "Don't worry," he called back. "The ankylosaur just eats plants."

Relieved, Grady stepped out of the shadows and moved toward the ankylosaur, which stood half in and half out of the swampy stream.

"But watch out for his tail," Max added—too late. The ankylosaur's massive, ball-tipped tail went *swish*. Grady dropped facedown in the mud—just in time. A split second later and the tail would have collided with his head. The ankylosaur waddled a few steps, and Grady slowly arose from the muck. His face and clothes were plastered with putrid, brown swamp-slime. Max zoomed in on Grady.

"Eeeww!" Allie said, grimacing. "That's so-o-o gross!"

"Thanks for the warning, McCrane," Grady said sarcastically. He flung gobs of mud from his face.

"Sorry," Max said. He swung the camcorder back to the ankylosaur, which was still trying to make friends with the orange Beetle. The creature rubbed its head against the driver's side door, and the mirror on the door broke off. The car sank deeper into the mire.

"Max," Allie said, "shouldn't we shoo that thing away?"

"If you want to, go right ahead," Max said. "But I'm not going near that thing. An ankylosaur may not eat people, but if it steps on you, you'll be just as dead." He lowered the camcorder. "Nuts! The camcorder died. My dad never remembers to charge the battery. He's so absent-minded."

Allie nervously scanned the clearing. "Max," she said, "as soon as that thing goes away, let's go home. This has been fun—but what if a pack of Velociraptors shows up?"

"Not a chance," Max said. "This is prehistoric North America. Velociraptors lived only in Asia."

"But what about other predators? It's not safe here."

"Good point," Max said. "There was *one* really nasty meat-eater in North America around this time—"

Thump!

The ground shuddered.

Max gulped and finished his sentence: "*Tyrannosaurus rex.*"

Thump! . . . Thump!

Up the hill, the herd of Stegocerases bolted in panic, melting into the forest. At the bottom of the hill, the anky-losaur turned and charged through a stand of tall ficus. Its entire bulk vanished from sight within moments.

Wild-eyed, Toby jumped up and dashed down the hill to join Max and Allie. "What's that?" he shouted, beads of sweat dotting his pudgy face.

Thump! . . . THUMP!

"Hey, McCrane!" Grady called from the swamp. "Do you hear that?"

"Quiet!" Max hissed. "Stand still!" The tone of urgency

in his voice convinced Grady, Allie, and even Toby to obey. No one moved.

Then they saw it: Tyrannosaurus rex.

Its heavy tread shuddered the earth as it stalked beyond a fringe of palm trees at the top of the hill. Its massive reptilian head rose over the treetops. It had daggerlike teeth, rippling jaw muscles, fierce predator eyes, and pebbly, leathery skin. The only sound it made was the terrible thunder of its footsteps. The beast took no notice of the four human beings who stood frozen in their tracks a mere fifty yards down the hill.

THUMP! . . . THUMP!

Then the great head turned toward them. The hungry reptile eyes stared directly at them. Allie fought down the scream in her throat.

"Max," she whispered. "Look at it! It's—"

"Shhh!" Max said.

"But Max," she whispered, "it's *purple!*" There was an edge of giggly lunacy in Allie's voice.

5

STRANDED IN TIME

Max worried that the fear was pushing Allie's mind over the edge. Horrified, he pictured her collapsing in a fit of hysterical laughter while the tyrannosaur pounced on them, a roaring frenzy of hot breath and ripsaw teeth. Keeping his own teeth clenched, Max hissed, "Con . . . trol . . . your . . . self!"

That seemed to do it. Allie went silent and stood completely still.

But she was right about one thing: The tyrannosaur *was* purple. Scared as he was, Max couldn't help being amazed at the wild profusion of dinosaur colors he had seen: green-and-yellow Stegocerases, an orange ankylosaur, and now a purple Tyrannosaurus rex! For a moment, he wondered if he was dreaming in Technicolor—but no, the sights, sounds, and smells were too intense, too detailed. As crazy as it all seemed, this was reality, not a dream.

And why shouldn't dinosaurs come in all the colors of the rainbow? Max and his friends were the first human beings to ever see dinosaurs in the flesh. Paleontologists— dinosaur experts—had only seen fossils, mostly bones. Even when paleontologists studied fossilized dinosaur skin, it was impossible to tell what color the skin had been when the dinosaur was alive. But Max was seeing something most paleontologists would give their right arm for: *a purple* Tyrannosaurus rex!

The dinosaur looked away—but then the worst possible thing happened: Toby fainted and fell facedown on the grass.

The tyrannosaur's head whipped back in their direction. It had noticed the motion of Toby's falling body. To a Tyrannosaurus rex, motion meant *food*. The creature's gustlike breaths shook the palm branches.

To his horror, Max felt his nose itch. He tried contorting his face to stop the itching. It only got worse.

"Max!" Allie whispered.

"Shhh!" Max hissed back.

"It sees us!"

"Shhh!"

Why couldn't Allie stand still and be quiet?! Why couldn't his nose stop itching?! Why hadn't they returned to their own time when they still had the chance?!

Screeeeee! Screeeeee!

Max didn't dare move his head, but he shifted his eyes

skyward. The pteranodons had returned. They slowly circled against the blue Cretaceous sky.

Distracted by the flying reptiles, the tyrannosaur turned and took a step—*THUMP!*—and blundered into the palm trees, sending one of them toppling over. Instantly, a blur of green-and-yellow motion stampeded out of hiding among the trees. It was the herd of Stegocerases, startled out of their hiding place by the crash of the palm tree. With a frenzied pounding of three-toed feet, the Stegocerases bolted helter-skelter across the clearing. Some dashed straight down the hill toward the humans.

"No, not this way!" Allie pleaded uselessly. "Go the other way!" In the next instant, she screamed and covered her face as several green-and-yellow dinos thundered around her.

The purple tyrannosaur roared hungrily at the sight of the Stegoceras stampede. Here was *food,* scattering in all directions! The dinosaur crashed through the trees and snapped its jaws at anything that moved.

"Run!" Max shouted. "Everybody to the car!"

Max was about to dash for the VW himself when he remembered Toby, lying in the tall grass. He rushed to Toby's side and rolled him over, ducking as a Stegoceras bounded, kangaroo-like, over them. "Toby!" Max screamed into the unconscious boy's face, grabbing the front of his shirt and shaking him.

Toby's eyes snapped open. His pasty face turned red with rage. "Let go of me, you dork!" he shouted.

"Come on," Max shouted back, "unless you want to end up inside that thing!" He pointed toward the raging purple dinosaur.

Toby saw the towering monster—and *screamed!* The tyrannosaur roared, its jaws descending on the back of a fleeing Stegoceras. There was a loud crunching sound and a high-pitched reptilian shriek—then the T. rex lifted the wriggling Stegoceras in its jaws.

Neither Toby nor Max stayed to watch. Both followed Allie downhill toward the VW Beetle, running as fast as their feet would carry them. Grady, covered in mud, dived through the passenger side as Allie, Max, and Toby reached the driver's side. They piled into the car and slammed the doors.

All four time travelers had taken refuge inside the car—but they were far from safe. Their breathing was a chorus of short, frantic gasps. Max was wheezing like a broken accordion. He dug his inhaler from his pocket, fumbled and almost dropped it, then took a quick puff. Then he panicked.

"Where's the camcorder?" he asked. "I must have left it out there!"

"It's on the strap around your neck!" Allie answered. "Get us out of here, Max!"

"Look out!" Grady shouted from the rear. "It's coming this way!"

The tyrannosaur had burst into the clearing and stood at

the top of the hill. Before, the beast had been half-hidden behind the trees, but now its entire bulk was visible, from head to tail. Its arms were almost ridiculously tiny, only a yard long, ending in small, two-clawed hands. Its legs, however, were massive and powerful, capable of supporting its six-ton weight. Each foot was equipped with three wickedly clawed toes plus a sharp dewclaw at the rear. The monster's stiff, pointed tail swung behind it, occasionally batting a tree to the ground—yet the beast didn't even notice.

Max, Allie, and Grady couldn't take their eyes off the creature. But Toby, crouched next to Grady and buried his head in his arms, blubbering hysterically.

"Allie! Switch on the power!" Max ordered as he laid the keyboard across his knees.

Allie opened the glove box and flipped the power switch. In the corner of Max's keyboard, a tiny yellow light flickered—then went dark.

"What!" Max said, tapping the keyboard. "What happened to the power? Those are brand-new batteries! They've got to work!" He glanced at the open glove box—then did a double take when he noticed the batteries in the battery rack: Energizers! He distinctly remembered putting in fresh Duracells just before they left!

"What's wrong, Max?" Allie said.

Max reached over and grabbed the spent batteries out of the rack. "These batteries!" he said. "They're dead!"

"Then so are we!" Allie cried.

"I saw you put in brand-new batteries, McCrane," Grady said. "Who could have—?"

The same thought hit Max, Allie, and Grady at the same instant. They turned and shouted, "*Toby!*"

Toby hid behind his hands. "Dude! It's not my fault! McCrane should have brought extra batteries!"

Ahead, the dinosaur bent down, eyeing the VW. Allie screamed. The T. rex heard and came for a closer look.

THUMP! . . . THUMP! . . . THUMP! . . .

The car rattled and shook. The windows went dark as a shadow passed over Timebender. In the seat next to Max, Allie sat as still as possible, though her body was shaking. Her lips moved silently. She was praying.

Grady's face was tilted upward, as if he were trying to see through the roof of the car. Beads of sweat glistened on his face.

Max looked to his left, out the driver's side window, and saw nothing but bumpy purple skin—the tyrannosaur had planted one leg just two feet from the door. He looked to his right, past Allie's frozen, wide-eyed face, and saw more purple skin—the tyrannosaur's other leg. The beast was straddling the car, standing directly over them! Looking out the windshield, he saw the creature's mighty tail swishing slowly back and forth.

The dinosaur took another lumbering step. Its foot

brushed the side of the car with a leathery, slithery sound. Allie gave a startled shriek, and the car slid even deeper into the muck. Water seeped in around the doors.

THUMP! . . . THUMP! . . . THUMP! . . . Thump! . . .

The heavy sound of the tyrannosaur's footsteps faded.

"It's leaving!" Allie whispered excitedly. "It didn't eat us!"

"Yeah," Max whispered back, "but we're still stuck here. Look, did any of you guys bring a flashlight, a CD player, a Game Boy—*anything* with batteries? Grady? Allie?"

They shook their heads—no.

"Toby?"

Toby Brubaker's pasty, dirt-streaked face appeared over the back of the seat. "Bringing the batteries was your job, McCrane," he accused in a shaky voice.

Max's face darkened. "Yeah," he said through clenched teeth, "and *sabotaging* the batteries was your job!"

Allie's face brightened. "I know! The battery in your camcorder!"

"You mean the one my dad forgot to charge?" Max asked. "It's dead, remember?"

Her face fell. "Oh, yeah." Seconds passed, then Allie brightened again. "The car battery?"

"There isn't any," Max said. "When my dad and I bought this car at the junkyard, there was no motor, no battery—just a body and wheels."

"Figure something out, McCrane!" Toby snapped. "I'm hungry! If the dinosaurs don't eat us, we're going to starve to death!"

Allie rolled her eyes. "How can you think of food at a time like this?"

"Toby, if you're that hungry," Max said with heavy sarcasm, "go pick some ginkgo fruit and quit complaining—" He stopped, his eyes widening. "Hey! That's it!"

"What's it?" Grady asked.

"Ginkgo fruit!"

"You're going to *eat* those smelly things?" Allie asked.

"No!" Max said. "I'm going to make *batteries* out of them!"

"He's losing it!" Grady said.

"I need pennies!" Max said.

"Pennies?" Allie said. "What for?"

"There's no time for questions," Max said. "Just give me all your pennies!"

"I've got some in my purse—," Allie began, then she grimaced. "No! I left my purse on the table in your lab!"

Grady checked his pockets. "I've got a quarter, two dimes, and a five-dollar bill. Here, you can have it all," he said, offering the money.

"No good! I need pennies!" Max said. "Toby! Empty your pockets!"

"All right, all right," Toby said. "I've got four pennies— but you have to pay me back!"

"You'll get your four cents back," Max said in an irritated voice. "Give them to me."

Toby held out the pennies, and Max snatched them.

"This is stupid," said Toby. "Who ever heard of making batteries out of fruit and pennies?"

"It's not stupid; it's science," said Max. "All you need to make electricity is some zinc and some fruit with acid in it—lemons or oranges work great. I've never tried it with ginkgo fruit, but it should work."

"But what are the pennies for?" Allie asked.

"Pennies are made of zinc," Max said.

"Yeah, right!" snorted Toby. "Everybody knows pennies are made of copper."

"They stopped making pennies out of copper in 1982," Max explained. "Now they make pennies out of zinc with a thin copper coating. We just have to scrape some of that copper away, and we'll have four shiny zinc electrodes for our batteries. You stick a zinc electrode in one side of the fruit and a copper electrode—like copper wire—in the other. The zinc reacts with acid in the fruit, and electrons move from the zinc electrode to the copper electrode. That's electrical current we can use to power Timebender."

"McCrane," said Grady, "you and Allie can stay here and scrape the copper coating off those pennies. Brubaker and I will go pick some ginkgo fruit."

Toby's face went white with fear. "No way! I'm not going out there!"

"Come on, Brubaker," Grady said. "You got us into this mess. The least you can do is help get us out. And McCrane, this idea of yours better work."

Max looked at Grady over his thick, round glasses. "If I can build a time machine out of an old Volkswagen," he said, "I can build a battery out of a piece of fruit."

Allie opened the door and pulled the seat forward to let the boys out. Grady and Toby squeezed through. Allie slammed the door and rolled down the window. "Be careful, guys," she said.

Allie helped Max search the car. They found a few scraps of copper wire that Max had left over from wiring the dashboard. They also found a screwdriver that Max had left under the seat, and a nail file that a previous owner of the VW had left under a floor mat. It was everything they needed. Max used the screwdriver to scratch the copper coating off two of the pennies; Allie scratched at the other two with the nail file.

Max wrapped the pennies with wire—just two loops around the "equator" of each penny. The wire had to make contact with the penny in order to make an electrical connection, while leaving enough zinc exposed to generate electricity. Then Max connected the other end of the wire to the computer keyboard.

Soon Toby and Grady returned with their hands full of ginkgo fruit.

"This is the dumbest thing I ever heard of," Toby

grumbled as he followed Grady into the car. "A fruit-powered time machine."

Max selected four of the ripest pieces of fruit and poked holes in them with the screwdriver.

Allie held her nose. "Are you about done?" she asked. "Those things really stink."

"Almost done," Max said. "I just have to—Did you hear that?"

Everyone froze and listened. It was faint, but unmistakable:

Thump! . . . Thump! . . . Thump!

Allie gasped. "Oh, hurry, Max! Hurry, hurry!"

Fingers shaking, Max worked faster, pushing the wire-wrapped pennies deep into the fruit. The circuit was complete. Max grabbed the keyboard—and his heart leaped with joy! The light on the keyboard was bright and steady. "We have power!" Max announced.

Allie, Grady, and Toby cheered!

"Shhh!" Max hissed. "Hear that?"

They listened again.

Thump! . . . Thump! . . . THUMP! . . . THUMP!

"It's coming this way!" Grady said.

Toby moaned and hid his head.

"Max," Allie pleaded, "get us out of here *now!*"

"I don't know the time coordinates!" Max said. "I need time to—"

Thump! . . . THUMP! . . . THUMP! . . . THUMP! . . .

A shadow fell all around them.

Allie's voice rose to a scream. "Now, Max! *Now!*"

Allie's scream was answered by a reptile scream, hungry and primal, from a throat as deep as a well. A huge inhuman face appeared in front of the windshield. Its eyes were red and unblinking. Teeth the size of a human arm dripped saliva. The jaws opened, revealing a glistening pink gullet that seemed bottomless.

The tyrannosaur *saw* them.

As Max stared into those brutish eyes, he forgot what he had to do. He froze with his hands poised over the keyboard.

"Max!" Allie shouted. "Now, Max!"

Max didn't move.

In front of them, the dinosaur head disappeared from view.

"Where did it go?" Grady asked. "What's it doing?"

Allie snatched the keyboard off Max's lap and tapped frantically on the keypad. The numbers she chose were completely random. Allie had no idea if the coordinates she typed would take them into the past or the future—and she didn't care. The numbers moved across the calculator displays. "Help us, God!" she pleaded, hitting the ENTER key.

Nothing happened. Nothing changed. They were still in the Cretaceous Period. Timebender wasn't working!

There was a horrible grinding sound—the sound of massive teeth clashing against metal. The roof of the Volkswagen went *crunch* as the dinosaur chomped on it. Windows broke and glass flew. The four time travelers screamed. They felt a sickening lurch in their stomachs as the car was yanked out of the mud and lifted into the air in the jaws of the tyrannosaur.

The beast had never bitten into metal before, and it didn't like the feeling of metal against its teeth. It shook the car back and forth, and the passengers tumbled inside like rag dolls.

"Please, God, please!" Allie screamed as she was tossed hard against the roof of the car, then slammed back into her seat.

The dinosaur tilted the car so that its nose pointed straight at the ground. Then the T. rex opened its jaws, releasing the Volkswagen. The car was free-falling from the height of a four-story building. Through the windshield, the four young time travelers saw the ground rushing to meet them—

And they knew they were going to die.

6

THE SPACE EMISSARY

The ground disappeared.

The entire *world* disappeared.

All around Timebender, there was nothing but space and stars. The Volkswagen was slowly tumbling through space.

It was dark inside Timebender. There was no light to see by except the faint light of the stars and the even fainter light from the keyboard and calculator displays. Max stared at the universe beyond the windows of the VW Beetle—a brilliant, star-frosted sky that slowly wheeled around them.

"Max!" Allie said breathlessly. "What happened! Where are we?"

"I don't know where we are—or when. I just know we timebended."

"But how?" Allie asked. "When I hit ENTER nothing happened! I don't get it!"

"Don't you remember?" Max said. "It takes ten seconds for Timebender to charge its capacitors before timebending." He hesitated, looking away. "Allie," he said guiltily, "I froze. I was so scared I just couldn't move. If you hadn't grabbed the keyboard—"

"Forget it, Max," Allie said. "We're all scared. It's just a good thing we all have each other to rely on."

"Max," Grady said, "why are we breathing? We're in space—and there's no air in space."

"Ohmygosh, Max!" Allie said. "Grady's right! The car windows are broken! There shouldn't be any air—but we're still alive!"

"Even if the T. rex hadn't broken the windows," Max said, "this old junker isn't airtight. I can only think of one explanation: a time discontinuity."

"A discount what?" Allie asked.

"Dis . . . con . . . tin . . . uity," Max said slowly. "A temporary disruption between our own time field and the time field of surrounding space. My guess is that it will last until the fruit batteries run out of power—and then all the air will blow out."

"And we'll die," Allie said.

"No!" Grady said, slapping the back of the seat with both hands. "Timebend us out of here! We don't know where we'll end up, but it's better than waiting to die!"

"You're right!" Max said. He grabbed the keyboard from Allie and punched in some random numbers on the keypad. The coordinates came up on the calculator display. He hit ENTER.

Allie scrunched her eyes shut. "God, please get us home!"

Max checked his wristwatch. "Six . . . five . . . four . . ."

The light on the keyboard dimmed.

"Oh, no!" Max said.

The light on the keyboard went dark. They were out of power.

Space exploded in blinding light. Directly in front of them, they saw the—the *what?* They had never seen anything like it. Shaped like a sphere, it gave off a brilliant golden light, as bright as the Sun—yet it didn't hurt their eyes to look at it. The object was directly in front of them, and it seemed to control Timebender's motion through space. The Volkswagen Beetle's tumbling slowed, then stopped. The shining sphere moved toward Timebender, engulfing the car and its passengers in its golden light.

The light was too beautiful for words. It shone inside the car, illuminating everything with a supernatural radiance. Their faces gleamed like the faces of angels. Their skin was as bright as molten metal. Their eyes glowed like sunlight reflected in white gold.

"This must be heaven," Allie said. There was no fear in her voice—only wonder.

"I don't think so," Max said. "I've never heard of Volkswagens in heaven."

"I want to stay here forever," Allie said.

"I want to go home," Toby whimpered.

"I want to look around," Grady said. "Let's go."

They got out of the car and stared at the VW Beetle in wonder: Even as crunched, dented, and broken as it was, the little car seemed majestic and glorified, an artist's masterpiece cast in pure gold.

"What is this place?" Allie asked.

"Maybe a spaceship," Max said. "Somehow the aliens knew we were in trouble. This ship came and surrounded us, took us aboard, and saved our lives."

"I don't think this is a spaceship," Grady said. "I don't know what this thing is, but it's not a machine."

"Grady's right," Allie said. "Look around you. There's nothing machinelike about it."

What was it, then? Whatever it was, it was filled with light—a light that seemed to come not from any single source, but from everywhere at once. As the four time travelers walked away from the car, they seemed to be walking on light, passing through light, breathing light, touching light. What's more, Max had a growing impression that this thing, whatever it was, was *watching* them. He decided to communicate with it.

"Hello!" Max said.

"Hello, Max," it answered.

Max jumped. Allie gasped. Grady's heart hammered against his rib cage. Toby stumbled backward in fear.

The voice was deep and resonant. Like the light, it seemed to issue from everywhere at once. "Please," the voice said, "don't be afraid. You are safe here."

A being seemed to form out of the light, gradually taking humanlike shape as it moved toward them. The momentary fear that Max, Allie, and Grady had felt simply melted away, replaced by a sense of awe that drove them to their knees. Only Toby still hung back in fear.

"Get off your knees," the light-being said. "You should not fear me, nor should you worship me. I am not the One who is worthy of your worship. I am merely one of His servants."

Max stood and examined the light-being closely. The shape of the being was like that of a man, but Max had the impression that there were more dimensions to this being than the three normal dimensions of height, width, and depth.

"Who are you?" Max asked.

"I am an Emissary of Elyon the Most High," the light-being replied. "Call me Gavriyel."

"Gavriyel," Max said, "we're time travelers, and we've gotten lost. Can you tell me what year this is?"

"You are outside of time. Your world does not yet exist.

Your question about time has no meaning here. I know you have many questions, Max. So do you, Allie, Grady, and Toby."

Allie and Grady appeared surprised and pleased that the Emissary knew their names. Toby merely looked pale and scared.

"How did you know our names?" Allie asked. "It's as if you were expecting us—but that's impossible. We came here by accident."

"Elyon the Most High sees all moments at once," Gavriyel said. "Events that surprise you are known to Him from the beginning of time. So your arrival here was no surprise. Your rescue, no accident."

"You mean," Grady said, "we thought we came here by accident, but you knew we were coming all along?"

"*He* knew," Gavriyel corrected.

"Hey!" Toby shouted. "You've got to send me home! I didn't want to come here."

The Emissary radiated gentle laughter. "Toby, lies are transparent here. You are here because of the choices you have made, and you will not return home until it is time for you to leave. The testing of your souls is about to begin."

Allie gulped. "The testing of our souls? That sounds dangerous."

"Oh, yes," Gavriyel said. "It will be very dangerous. Your souls will be in great peril."

"There must be some mistake," Max pleaded. "We're

four scared, lost . . . *kids!* We'll just make a mess of things."

"Everything you say is true, Max," Gavriyel said. "But it pleases the Most High to use the small things to confound the great, the weak things to confound the mighty, the foolish things to confound the wise."

Grady turned to Allie and Max. "Look, guys, what if we just refuse to go?" He turned to the Emissary with a look of defiance. "You can't *make* us go on this test thing! Don't we have a choice to say yes or no?"

"You already made your choice," Gavriyel said, "when you stepped aboard your time machine. Elyon did not force you to come here. It was a decision each of you made of your own free will. All choices have consequences. When you left your own time, you accepted the risk of going wherever the currents of time might take you. Those currents have taken you into the middle of a great war. It is too late to turn back."

"War!" Toby exclaimed. "What kind of war?"

"A war more terrible than you can imagine. Look!"

In the next instant, the golden enclosure that surrounded them became as transparent and insubstantial as a soap bubble. The time travelers, the Emissary, and the Volkswagen appeared to be traveling in open space, supported by nothing. All around them, the endless sky sparkled with stars and glowed with luminous dust clouds.

Allie pointed out into space. "What are those?"

Where she pointed, a swirling mass of golden lights was approaching. There were thousands of them, like sparks from bursts of fireworks. As they came closer, their shape became obvious. They were golden spheres of light, like the one that had rescued them in space.

"We are being joined by legions of Emissaries like me," Gavriyel said. "The forces of Elyon are preparing for war."

The four young humans were about to be plunged into a *war*—a war in the depths of space, in the abyss of time. Two cosmic armies would clash over one prize—the universe itself.

7

Battle Before Time

"All around you are the forces of Elyon," Gavriyel said.

The shining spheres surrounded them above and below, and on every side—like thousands and thousands of golden suns, flying in formation. Max tried to make scientific sense of what he saw.

Perhaps the Emissaries were beings of a different dimension. Max remembered that some scientists claimed the universe consists of nine dimensions of space and one dimension of time. Could the Emissaries belong to one of those higher dimensions? If so, was one of those dimensions a *spiritual* dimension? Or were the Emissaries simply beyond scientific explanation?

And what about Gavriyel's sphere—this strange globe of nothingness that carried them through the universe at the speed of astonishment? Gavriyel had caused the walls of the golden sphere to become invisible without a word or a command or a wave of his arms. Did he do it with a thought?

In fact, Max had come to think of Gavriyel's sphere as "the bubble." From within Gavriyel's spirit-bubble, Max could see in all directions to an infinite distance. Everywhere he looked, he saw *wonders:* a blue nebula left behind by the death of a star. A black hole—an eddy of violet-colored gases swirling down a storm drain of intense gravity. Two spiral galaxies in collision, their shapes distorted by vast tidal forces. Most of all, Max saw stars—billions of them—like nuclear-powered gemstones shining in every color of the rainbow.

Standing within Gavriyel's spirit-bubble, gazing at the wonders of the universe, Max felt a thrill of wonder over the beauty of the universe all around him.

Max was absorbed in his thoughts when Allie pointed ahead. "Look, Max," she said. "There's a star straight ahead. I think we're slowing down."

Max looked where Allie pointed. One star among the millions was growing in size and brilliance, becoming a sun, round and yellow. Soon, Max noticed a number of planets slowly and majestically circling the star. As the spirit-bubble moved toward the center of the solar system, a wispy-tailed comet sailed past.

"There!" Grady said, pointing. "That's Earth! We're going home!" The planet Grady pointed to looked achingly familiar—a blue-white marble with a single moon. The time travelers instantly felt homesick when they saw it.

Then Max said, "It looks like Earth, but it can't be. Our Earth doesn't exist yet."

"You're right, Max," said Gavriyel. "Elyon calls that world Alanthe."

"Does anyone live there?" Grady asked.

"There are living creatures on that world," Gavriyel said, "but no people, no intelligent life. Alanthe is much like the world your Earth will be. It has oceans, land, air, clouds, plants, and animals. That is why the Enemy seeks to destroy all such worlds. He knows that the Eternal Plan will be carried out on a planet like that one—but he doesn't know which one. So he tries to destroy them all."

Allie pointed to a mass of glowing red lights that swarmed into the solar system. "What are those?" she asked.

Gavriyel was somber. "Those," he said, "are the forces of the Enemy. The battle has begun."

As they drew closer to the red fleet of the Enemy, the four time travelers could see that the Enemy forces were glowing spheres, just like the spheres of the Emissaries. The only difference was that the Enemy spheres glowed with red light instead of gold.

The two forces collided around the blue-white planet, Alanthe, with crackling flashes of energy and massive explosions. Golden spirits clashed with crimson spirits in pitched battles of light versus darkness. Space was split by screams of spirits that fell like meteors through the atmosphere of Alanthe. The four humans held their ears, but couldn't shut out those screams, which came not as sound, but as waves of soul-force.

The golden legions of Elyon were superior in strength and number. They beat the red legions back and sent them reeling in a dazed retreat.

Allie and Max cheered, but Gavriyel said, "Wait! Don't celebrate yet. The Enemy is crafty. The battle is far from won."

The Enemy's red fleet retreated toward the sun—but the retreat turned out to be nothing more than a devious form of attack. Gavriyel was right—the Enemy was crafty. The Enemy's forces swirled in a tight orbit around the yellow star. As they circled the star, its fiery surface churned. It grew brighter and whiter, sending out crackling streamers of nuclear fire.

The golden forces responded, attacking the red forces of the Enemy, blasting the evil spirits with energies beyond human imagination. Some of the Enemy's forces were scattered by the Emissaries' attack, but the remaining forces continued to assault the star.

Flash!

The star *exploded* in blinding cascades of light. A shock wave of energy and star-stuff blasted outward, torching each planet it passed. The wave of fire and energy engulfed the blue-white world—

And when the wave had passed, Alanthe was a blackened cinder.

Allie screamed.

Max fell to his knees. "No!" he shouted.

Behind Max and Allie, Grady and Toby were stunned.

"All those planets were destroyed!" Max said. "You said there was life on Alanthe! But now—"

"That is the Enemy we face," Gavriyel said. "He is a hater and a destroyer."

"But how can Elyon allow it to happen?" Allie asked, her tears flowing freely. "Didn't Elyon love that world? Doesn't He have the power to destroy evil before it happens?"

"Elyon is the source of all love," Gavriyel said. "And all power belongs to Him. But there are reasons why the Enemy and his Dark Emissaries are allowed to do what they do. It is all part of the Eternal Plan."

"The Eternal Plan!" Allie exclaimed. "That planet is dead! Doesn't that matter to Elyon?"

Gavriyel turned away and gazed out into the universe. The stars wheeled dizzyingly as the bubble tilted toward the blackened husk of Alanthe. The kids could see that the atmosphere of the murdered planet boiled with soot-laden gases.

Gavriyel turned to Allie. "You think Elyon is not wounded to the heart when even *one* of His creatures dies? How little you understand His heart. You don't know how much pain an infinite heart must feel! You can't imagine how it must hurt to absorb the pain of an entire universe."

Allie bit her lip. "But if He cares," she asked, "and if He hurts so much, then why does He allow those evil things to exist?" She pointed out into space, where the red swarm billowed away from the glowing remains of the destroyed star.

Grady stepped forward, his face twisted in anger. "Allie's right," he said. "If Elyon is as powerful as you say, this war could be over—just like *that!*" He snapped his fingers. "Explain it to me, Gavriyel! Explain why Elyon allows things like war! Explain why He allows people to suffer! Explain—" His voice faltered, and his eyes brimmed with tears. "Explain why my dad had to get sick and die!"

Allie reached out and put her arm around Grady.

"You ask a reasonable question," Gavriyel said at last. "And you shall have an answer."

Grady's eyes came alight with hope. "Yeah?"

"But not now," Gavriyel said.

"What!" Grady pulled away from Allie. "Why *not* now?"

"Because I do not know the future," Gavriyel said. "Only Elyon Himself knows all things. I can only tell you what He chooses to reveal to me. The rest will be revealed to you in time."

The bubble turned and accelerated in a new direction, leaving the ruined star system behind.

"What you are about to see," the Emissary said, "is to prepare you for your time of testing. These things will take place at an altered rate of temporal flow."

Allie had a questioning look. "An altered what?"

"I think Gavriyel means," Max said, "that he's going to show us things at a faster speed, like fast-forwarding a videotape."

"Yes," the spirit-being said. "Thousands of years of cosmic war will be compressed into a few minutes of human time. Watch."

The stars sped past. The golden forces of Elyon and the red forces of the Enemy swirled from one star system to the next. They clashed, retreated, and clashed again. Incredible energies exploded in space. Comets were dislodged from their cold orbits and flung at planets. Worlds were torn from their paths and sent colliding into neighboring worlds. Stars flared into blinding supernovas. Other stars contracted into black holes—vast gravity fields that ripped space and time apart. The four humans didn't want to watch, but they couldn't pull their eyes away.

"Is this some kind of movie," Max asked in a hushed voice, "or is this really happening?"

"It is happening just as you are seeing it," the Emissary replied, "but at an accelerated rate."

"How can you do that?" Max said. "How do you make time speed up or slow down?"

"In Elyon's realm, a thousand years can be like a day, or

a day like a thousand years. All of time is His to command. Look—we are coming to a crucial moment."

A bright yellow star came into view directly in front of them. Though the star was very small and distant, each of the four felt it—a sense of recognition, a sense that they were *home*.

"That's our sun, isn't it?" Max said.

"Yes," the Emissary said. "We are at the outer edges of your own solar system. Much time has passed since I rescued you in space."

"We're slowing down," Allie said.

"Our speed through space hasn't changed," Gavriyel said. "But I'm matching our time rate to the temporal flow of surrounding space."

"Look—planets!" Grady said. "That one's Saturn, isn't it? I can tell by the rings."

"And there's Jupiter," Max said, pointing to a large, banded world, "the largest planet in our solar system."

"Yes," Gavriyel said, "and if you look closely, you can see—"

"Mars!" Max said. "No, wait. That's Mars over there. I don't get it. There's a planet between the orbits of Mars and Jupiter. It shouldn't be there."

"Max, look!" Allie said. "The forces of the Enemy!"

Max looked where Allie pointed. High overhead, an evil swarm of crimson lights descended toward the solar system. Close behind them came a larger cloud of golden lights—the forces of Elyon. The red forces gathered on the mystery planet between Mars and Jupiter. They covered its cold, gray surface with an angry red glow. Even the night-side of the planet burned with the crimson glare of evil. The golden fleet surrounded the planet where the red forces had retreated to make their last stand.

"What happens now?" Allie asked.

"Something both terrible and wonderful," Gavriyel said.

Max and Allie exchanged questioning looks. They couldn't understand how something could be terrible and wonderful at the same time.

Then the universe was split by a white-hot radiance, like a bolt of lightning, but infinitely more powerful. The universe lit up from one end to the other. The sudden brilliance of the light wrenched a startled cry from the four human voyagers.

Max instantly realized that what he saw was scientifically impossible—light travels at 186,000 miles per second, and it would take millions of years for light to travel from one end of the universe to the other. This light had filled the whole universe in a single instant.

A Voice was in the light—a Voice that was felt in the soul, not heard with the ears. Max had no doubt that the Voice could be felt from one end of the universe to the other. It was a Voice of deep anger, but also of deep sorrow. No words could be understood, but Max felt that the Voice thundered with judgment and doom. His feelings were confirmed when he saw the red lights that covered the planet begin to seethe and stir. A mass wail of despair went up from the surface of the planet—and also a cry of defiance and rebellion.

The light that had brightened the universe slowly faded. The golden cloud of Elyon's forces parted and moved away from the planet. And then—

A searing bolt of white-hot light roared out of the heart of the universe. It streaked across the solar system and blasted the planet.

Allie screamed and turned away. The boys hid their faces.

The planet blew apart in millions of glowing fragments. Among the fragments and dust clouds of the shattered planet, the Enemy's scattered forces swirled like a swarm of hornets after their nest has been stirred. Pursued by the golden forces of Elyon, the red fugitives retreated toward the next planet sunward—the planet Mars.

"Another planet destroyed," Allie said, "this time, by Elyon Himself. Did anyone live on that planet?"

"It was a lifeless world," the Emissary said. "The only inhabitants were the forces of the Enemy who took a last desperate refuge there. But those evil spirits are not life as you understand it. They are Dark Emissaries—those who have rebelled against Elyon, and who no longer have the golden light of Elyon within them. Dark Emissaries are spirit-beings, as am I. They can be defeated—but they cannot be killed by simply blowing a planet apart."

"Hey!" Max said. "The asteroid belt!"

"The what?" Grady said.

"In our own time, there's a large group of asteroids between the orbits of Mars and Jupiter," Max said. "It's called the asteroid belt. We saw the creation of the asteroid belt when that planet was destroyed."

"Yes," Gavriyel said. "Those fragments of the shattered planet are a sign in the heavens of Elyon's judgment against the Enemy."

The spirit-bubble of Gavriyel sped onward, following the red swarm of Enemy forces as they retreated toward Mars. As the voyagers drew closer to Mars, it became clear that *this* Mars was not the "Red Planet Mars" they had learned about in school. It didn't look at all like the pictures of Mars in the science class textbooks. This Mars was a green-and-blue world, with swirls of white clouds in the atmosphere. In fact, it looked a lot like Earth. It had seas of liquid water, and its land masses were carpeted in lush, green plant life.

But as the red forces of the Enemy settled onto the surface of the planet, the land masses took on a scary red glow. The rebellious Dark Emissaries covered the land areas of Mars. The entire universe seemed to hold its breath.

"Will there be another attack?" Allie asked.

"No," Gavriyel said. "The war continues, but not in a way the Enemy expects."

As the golden forces of Elyon positioned themselves around the green planet of Mars, a flash of red light erupted from the center of one of the land masses. The flash became a spreading ring of fire, like the ripple a pebble makes when dropped in a pond. The wave of fire spread around to the far side of the planet, leaving blackened land and boiling seas wherever it passed. The fleecy white clouds in the Martian atmosphere turned into ugly stains of smoke. The green world became a charred wasteland.

Max, Allie, and Grady were horrified—but Toby chuckled darkly. He seemed to enjoy the terrible spectacle as if it were a mere fireworks display.

"What happened?" Allie asked.

"The Enemy has destroyed this beautiful world," Gavriyel explained, "because he hates Elyon's creations. He has reshaped this planet to his own liking. Elyon the Most High is the Creator; the Enemy is a destroyer."

"We've seen enough," Max said. "Please—let us go home now."

"No," the Emissary said. "Your way home leads through this world you call Mars."

"No!" Allie said, her eyes wide with horror. "You can't send us there! The Enemy is there!"

"That's true," Gavriyel said. "He hides under the surface of that world. But that is where you must go."

"Will it be dangerous down there?" Grady asked.

"There is always danger," Gavriyel said, "in the presence of the Enemy."

8

THE CAVES OF MARS

The bubble descended through layers of acid-yellow fumes and churning black clouds.

Like a soap bubble touching the ground, the spirit-bubble vanished upon contact with the soil of Mars. Gavriyel, the four young humans from Earth, and the battered old Volkswagen stood upon the ruined surface of the fourth planet from the sun. All around them, golden balls of light drifted downward, touched the ground, and were transformed into glowing spirit-beings like Gavriyel.

Under smoke-blackened skies, the Martian landscape was twilight-dark. What light there was came from Gavriyel and the other Emissaries.

"The air smells nasty!" Toby complained.

"Like smoke and sulfur," Allie said.

Max took a tentative breath, then he grimaced. "It's

breathable—but just barely." He checked his pocket and made sure his inhaler was ready—just in case.

They stood on the cracked, broken ground of a deep valley, surrounded by mountains. In some places, fires still burned. In others, curls of black smoke rose from the ground and ascended to the sky. A heavy smog overshadowed the jagged mountains that ringed the valley in steep ranks of cliff and crag.

Max noticed that when he walked, his footsteps crunched in the charred soil. Tufts of gray stubble covered much of the ground. That stubble—all that remained of the grass that had once covered the planet—turned to a powdery ash when trampled. The scorched planet seemed safe to walk on, even though the four young humans could feel heat radiating from the ground through the soles of their shoes.

A golden sphere sailed down from the sky and landed in front of Gavriyel. It touched the ground with a sparkling shimmer. In the next instant, there stood an Emissary unlike all the others who were gathered in the blackened valley. He was taller than the rest, and the golden light that poured from his face shone with a stormy intensity.

There was something strange and stern about this tall Emissary. Whereas Gavriyel seemed gentle and comforting, this newly arrived Emissary seemed fierce and forbidding. He had the look of a warrior about him. The four kids could not help feeling afraid in his presence.

The stern Emissary spoke. "Do not be afraid," he said. "I am Mikael, captain of the Legions of the Most High."

"These are the humans from out of time," Gavriyel said. "They are called Max, Allie, Grady, and Toby."

"Well," Mikael said. He sounded surprised—and faintly amused. "So *these* are humans. Hardly what I expected."

"That appears to be Elyon's intention," Gavriyel said. "If humans are not what *we* expect, they will not be what the Enemy expects, either."

"True," Mikael said. "The Eternal Plan is full of surprises."

Gavriyel turned to the four time travelers. "Well, my young friends, the time has come. Mikael shall introduce you to the Enemy."

"Come," Mikael said, pointing down the valley slope to a place of deep ravines and shadows. The way was dark and scary.

"Where are we going?" Max asked.

"To the cave of the Enemy," the Emissary captain replied.

Allie trembled. Max and Grady exchanged worried glances. No one moved.

"I'm not going," Toby said, scowling defiantly at Mikael. "You can't make me."

Mikael's voice was as sharp and cold as the edge of a sword. "Come!"

There was no more discussion. Mikael turned and started down the slope. All four followed—Max, then

Allie, Grady, and Toby. Gavriyel walked behind Toby, making sure he stayed with the group. The Emissary captain led the way across tumbled, blasted ground, and into a deep notch between two rock walls. As they passed through the shadows of the narrow crevice, Max heard Allie talking softly to herself: " . . . though I walk through the valley of the shadow of death, I will fear no evil, for You are with me. . . ."

The notch in the rocks opened out upon a wide ledge overlooking a deep canyon. Mikael, Gavriyel, and the four travelers came out onto the ledge. Beyond the ledge was an alarming drop of hundreds of feet to the bottom of the canyon. A natural stone bridge, erosion-carved, crossed the canyon to a jagged cave-cliff on the far side. Red fires burned at the bottom of the canyon, sending up sooty black plumes. There were several cave openings in the cliff across the canyon. Blood-red light and greasy black smoke poured from the large cave at the opposite end of the stone bridge.

Max looked to the right and left, and saw row after row, rank after rank, of golden Emissaries standing on high bluffs overlooking the canyon. The vast armies of Elyon had gathered to confront the Enemy.

Mikael turned to face the humans. "The Enemy," he said, "is a destroyer, a murderer, and a deceiver. He hates all that is good, including the beauty of creation. He has destroyed this world. Can you bear to see what it once looked like?"

The boys made no answer, but Allie stepped forward. "I want to see," she said.

Mikael turned and faced the canyon. He raised his arms, and a wave of golden light radiated from him, changing the entire landscape. The grimy, smoke-stained sky became a clear, crystalline dome of intense blue-violet. Wispy pale-blue clouds floated high in the atmosphere. The smoking canyon became a lush ravine, teeming with life. Its stone walls hung with creeping vines bearing broad purple leaves and huge snow-white blossoms. Starfishlike animals with transparent blue bodies crawled among the white vine-flowers, feeding on nectar. The stone bridge was draped in green mosses and purple vines. Tall grasses carpeted the ledge, clung to cracks in the surrounding rocks, and painted the valley a fluorescent green all the way to the steep purple mountains. In the air overhead, blue jellyfish-like creatures floated gently in the Martian breeze—living kites that trailed long green streamers.

The scene was so wonderful that, for a moment, the four young humans forgot to take a breath.

Then Mikael's arms fell to his sides. The beautiful vision of a living Mars disappeared. The landscape became a wasteland of smoke and ash, blight and ruin once more.

Allie put her hands to her face and wept.

"Now you see," Mikael said, "what the Enemy has done to this world. Elyon has revealed this to you for a reason. Look at the death all around you. Look at the senseless loss of life and beauty. And *understand:* This is what the Enemy would do to your *souls.* Never forget what you have seen here today."

Mikael turned toward the caves across the canyon. The whole planet seemed to wait in terrible suspense. Then Mikael called out in a loud voice, "Lightbringer!"

His voice echoed away, down the smoking canyon, across the cracked and charred valley, and all the way to the blackened mountains. But no answer returned.

Mikael stepped onto the natural stone bridge. He walked out to the middle of the span and stopped. Again he called out in a loud voice, "Lightbringer!"

The echo of his voice rolled away like thunder. Deep within the largest cave, something stirred in the darkness and smoke.

Eyes wide behind his round glasses, Max turned to Gavriyel. "The Enemy's name is Lightbringer?" he asked in an astonished whisper. "How can something so evil be a light-bringer?"

"Before he turned against the Most High," Gavriyel said, "Lightbringer was the morning star, the son of the dawn—the most glorious of all the Emissaries of Elyon's realm. But in his rebellion, he became a thing of ugliness, horror, and darkness. The Light of Elyon no longer lives in the creature called Lightbringer."

Out on the stone bridge, Mikael called out once more. "Lightbringer! Answer me!"

A voice rumbled from the throat of the cave. "I hear you, Mikael."

Mikael spoke again—but his voice was filled with sadness rather than anger. "How you have fallen, Lightbringer."

"I am defeated," the Enemy said. "Is the *Most High* satisfied with my humiliation?" The words *Most High* dripped with mockery and bitterness.

"The Lord of Creation takes no joy in your destruction," Mikael said. "Nor do I. But this is only what you have brought upon yourself."

"Leave me, Mikael. Leave me to my regrets and my hate."

"You know what you must do," the captain of the Emissaries said.

"Never," the Enemy snarled. "I do not accept it."

"You must accept it," Mikael said. "The verdict of the Most High is true and just."

"There is no justice for me!" the Enemy raged. "I will *never* accept His judgment!"

"Do not blame the Most High for your eternal loss, Lightbringer," Mikael answered, his voice turning cold and stern. "You have done this to yourself—and you have led a third of the hosts of heaven to destruction."

"I begged you to join me!" the unseen Enemy roared from the smoking cave. "You, Gavriyel, and the rest! I call upon you now! You can still join me—and together we will rule the universe!"

Mikael shook his head in amazement, then turned and walked back to the ledge. "Sheer madness," he muttered sadly.

Max noticed a rhythmic whistling noise. When he realized it was his own breathing, he slipped the inhaler from his pocket and took a puff.

Gavriyel stepped forward and strode out upon the stone bridge. "Lightbringer," he called in a clear, strong voice.

There was a moment of startled silence. Then the shape of the Enemy could be seen at the mouth of the cave—a dim shape with red, glowing eyes, wreathed in smoke and gloom. "Ah, Gavriyel, *old friend,*" the Enemy said in a voice dripping with mockery and hate.

"Father of Lies," Gavriyel said, "don't call me 'friend.' Our friendship was over when you launched this doomed rebellion."

The Enemy's eyes flickered like flaming coals as he crept out of the cave, approaching the far end of the stone bridge. His form was vague and difficult to see through the smoke, but it gave a strong impression of being grossly disfigured. It seemed like something that had once been beautiful, but now was ruined and twisted.

"What are those . . . *things* . . . you have brought with you?" the Enemy asked. "They look like animals, but they seem . . . almost intelligent."

The four young time travelers huddled together behind Mikael, trying to hide from that awful stare.

"These creatures are called humans," Gavriyel said. "Don't be deceived by appearances. They may have animal-like bodies, but they are made in the image of Elyon Himself. You have much to learn about humans—but not here, not on this world."

The Enemy's eyes dimmed. "What do you mean?"

"Elyon has decreed that you and the rest of the rebellious ones are to leave this planet. You will be exiled on the third planet—the place called Earth."

The Enemy laughed slyly. "We are forbidden to go there," he said. "That world is sealed, and we cannot enter it."

"The seal has been lifted by order of the Most High," Gavriyel said. "You will be shut inside the boundaries of that world, and you will never be allowed to roam the universe again."

"I don't understand," the Enemy growled. "Elyon has already decreed that we should spend eternity in the Pit. Why does he send us to Earth?"

"The Pit still awaits you," Gavriyel said, "after the Last Judgment."

"Why?" the Enemy asked. "Why doesn't He simply send us to the Pit and be done with it?"

"All that the Lord of Creation does," Gavriyel said, "He does to fulfill the Eternal Plan."

"That is no answer."

"That is the only answer that has been given to me," Gavriyel said, "and to you."

The Enemy's hateful stare turned toward the humans. "What about *them?* What do *they* have to do with me? They are mortal and weak. They have soft animal bodies that are easily killed."

"You will one day see," Gavriyel said, "that Elyon has a great place for humans in the Eternal Plan."

"The Eternal Plan!" the Enemy snarled. "Why doesn't Elyon tell us plainly what His Plan is all about? Elyon's judgments are unfair and His will makes no sense! Tell your Master that I defy Him!"

"He knows that," Gavriyel said.

"Tell Him there will be more battlefields!"

"He knows that, too," Gavriyel said. "Battlefields named Eden, Golgotha, and Armageddon."

"Those names mean nothing to me!"

"They will," Gavriyel said. He turned and walked back to the ledge.

"Tell Him there will be more death, more destruction!" the Enemy roared at Gavriyel's back.

But Gavriyel had nothing more to say to the Enemy. Reaching Mikael and the four humans, he said, "Let's go." As they passed through the notch between the rock walls, they heard the Enemy roaring at their backs. His hate echoed along the canyon and across the valley.

"I'll destroy all He has created! Tell Him! This war is not over!"

As they came out of the crevice and trudged up the

slope, Max was trembling. "Gavriyel," he said as they reached the place where the orange Volkswagen stood upon the blistered ground, "what does the Enemy mean— 'this war is not over'? He was beaten, wasn't he?"

Gavriyel looked down at Max. Though his face could not be seen through the glow of golden light that surrounded him, Gavriyel seemed to radiate pity for the boy. "You don't understand, Max," he said. "The *real* war is just beginning—but the battlefield has shifted. This battle will no longer be fought among the stars, but among souls."

The golden bubble formed around Timebender and the four young time travelers. Along with thousands of other golden spheres, it lifted from the surface of Mars and floated into the blackened sky. The Enemy was still howling from his cave as the fleet of golden spirits departed the planet.

When the Emissaries of Elyon had left, a great wind rose up. It scoured the blackened surface of Mars, scrubbing away the soot and ash, revealing clean, red clay. The wind whirled through the canyons and whistled over the mountains of Mars. It sucked the evil spirits from their holes, caves, and hiding places, and it flung them screaming out into empty space.

The wind carried the evil spirits through a hundred million miles of cold vacuum, to a beautiful blue planet where no human had yet lived. There, on a world that would one day be known as Earth, the Enemy and the other rebellious spirits were exiled.

9

THE GARDEN AT THE DAWN OF THE WORLD

The battlefield has shifted. This battle will no longer be fought among the stars, but among souls. Gavriyel's words haunted Max as he gazed down upon the swirling surface of Mars. Max knew that Gavriyel had told him something truly terrible—and something terribly true: His own soul was about to become a battlefield. And so was Allie's soul. And Grady's. And Toby's. The thought filled Max with a fear he had never known before.

From the orbiting bubble, Max watched the supernatural winds cleanse the grimy blackness from the face of Mars. That planet was dead, demolished by the Enemy— but at least its scars had been scrubbed away. Thousands of years in the future, scientists would point their telescopes at Mars. They would see a Red Planet, and they wouldn't even suspect how green and alive it had once been.

But it wasn't the future of Mars that occupied Max's thoughts. He was thinking about his own future, and the future of his friends. He turned to Gavriyel. "Isn't there some way out of this?"

"You don't always get to choose your adventures," Gavriyel said. "Sometimes your adventures choose you. All you can do is face your test as best you can."

"At least tell us what to expect," Allie said.

"I will tell you what I can," the Emissary said. "You will go to Earth, where the Enemy has been exiled. There you will face him, and he will try to destroy your souls."

"No!" Allie said, her eyes wide. "How can we win against someone like *that?*"

"Yeah," Grady said. "What about the danger? The Enemy said something about *killing* us."

"Danger?" Toby sneered, wandering over to the Volkswagen. "What danger? I just figured it out. This whole weird trip is just a bad dream. I'm going to wake up, and all of you losers will be gone—as soon as I do *this!*" He launched a mighty kick at the driver's side door. "Yeow!" he yelped, hopping and grabbing his foot. "Okay," he snapped, "so it's a *realistic* dream."

"This isn't a dream, Toby," Allie said. "You'd better deal with it."

"Allie is right. This is reality," Gavriyel said. "And there is no guarantee that you will come through this test alive. The true goal of the Enemy is not to destroy you, but to deceive you. The victory he seeks is not to murder your body, but to murder your *soul*. The Enemy's greatest power, and your greatest danger, is that he will seem good and kind, and you will *want* to believe in him."

"Why would we want to believe in the Enemy?" Allie asked. "We've all seen the Enemy. We've seen how evil he is. We saw the stars and planets he destroyed. We've seen his eyes and heard his voice."

"Allie's right," Max said. "Us? Believe in him? No way!"

"The Enemy is a deceiver," Gavriyel said. "He can assume many pleasing shapes."

"He won't fool me," Allie said. "He can probably kill me with a snap of his fingers, but he can't fool me. I know the difference between good and evil."

"Sure," Grady said. "Everybody knows what evil looks like: Darth Vader, Dracula, Hitler. When we see the Enemy, we'll know."

"Put no trust in appearances," Gavriyel said. "Do not be overconfident."

"But *you'll* be with us," Max said. "You won't let the Enemy fool us."

"I cannot be with you," Gavriyel said.

"What?" Max exclaimed. "You can't just leave us alone against the Enemy! Against him, we're toast!"

"But that is what I'm trying to tell you," Gavriyel said. "If you try to face the Enemy in your own strength, you are—as you say—toast. So you must not face the Enemy alone. You must ask Elyon to go with you."

"But how can we ask Him?" Max said. "We've never seen Him."

"I think I know," Allie said. "We can talk to Him and He'll hear us—right?"

"Yes," Gavriyel said. "Of course."

"Guys," Allie said, "let's talk to Him together."

"Oh, I know what this is all about," Grady said, frowning. "Gavriyel, you want us to *pray,* right? Well, I've tried praying before. It doesn't work."

"You mean, when you prayed for your father?" Allie asked. "Grady, I know you think God let you down, but—"

"Forget it!" Grady said, folding his arms and leaning against the car. "Look, if you want to pray, go ahead. No one's stopping you. But count me out."

"Forget it, Allie," Max said. "You can't change his mind."

"Toby," Allie said, "come join us."

"Yeah, right!" Toby snickered. "Do I look like some kind of religious geek?" He climbed up on the hood of the Volkswagen, nursing his aching toe. "I'm just going to hang out right here until I wake up."

Max sighed. "Come on, Allie. I guess it's just you and me." Max and Allie went off behind the Volkswagen to pray by themselves.

Gavriyel turned to the other two boys. "Grady, Toby," he said, "I warn you—I beg you—do not face the Enemy alone."

Grady looked away. Toby made a rude noise, then laughed.

"I've done all I can do," Gavriyel said. "We will be on Earth soon."

A few minutes later, Max and Allie returned. "We're ready, Gavriyel," Allie said. "At least as ready as we can be."

The bubble descended toward Earth. The continents and coastlines looked very different from those of the twenty-first century.

"Since we left Mars," Gavriyel said, "only a few minutes have passed for us—but out there, on Earth, millennia have gone by. Even though you last saw the Enemy only minutes ago, you will not recognize him. And yet even though he last saw you thousands of years ago, he will recognize you instantly. That is all the warning I can give you."

"We'll remember," Max said. "And we'll be ready."

"No," Gavriyel said. "You won't remember. And you won't be ready. You will be deceived."

The four time travelers stepped onto the grass of Earth. They turned around in time to see Gavriyel waving good-bye and shimmering like a golden mirage upon the air. "Do not trust appearances!" he said. "Trust only in Him!"

"No!" Max called. "Don't go yet!"

But Gavriyel was already gone, and they were alone.

Timebender sat on the grass nearby, a battered orange Volkswagen with a crunched roof. It looked ridiculously out of place—in the Garden of Eden.

The air was as clear as crystal, as bright and sparkling as diamonds. The gently rolling hills were carpeted with thick, sweet-smelling grass and bordered by fragrant woods of acacia, cassia, jasmine, and sweet saso. In the distance, majestic snow-topped mountains rose to the heavens. From somewhere not far away came the sounds of a waterfall and a gurgling stream.

"Well, here we are," Max said. "Now what do we do?"

"Yeah," Allie said. "Do we, like, wait for the Enemy to show up? Or should we go looking for him?"

"I think we should at least look around," Grady said, "and see where we are." He brushed at the dried mud that caked his shirt and jeans. "Let's go this way. I hear running water. I need to wash this crudacious mud off me."

"It's Cretaceous," Max said.

"Whatever," Grady said. "Let's go."

With Grady in the lead, they began exploring the Garden at the Dawn of the World. They walked down a grassy slope and soon found themselves passing into the shade of a grove of fruit trees. The grove was wild and untended. The tree branches were heavy with red, ripe fruit of a kind they had never seen before. Allie was the first to pick one. It was round, with soft, red skin and juicy, pink flesh. She took a bite and pink juice dribbled down her chin. It was the most delicious fruit she had ever tasted. Soon, all four were eating and wiping their chins.

"Everything is so beautiful here," Allie said, "and the fruit is so sweet! How could there be any danger in this place?"

Max had finished one piece of fruit and started on another when a moving glint of silver caught the corner of his eye. He turned his head and peered at the edge of the grove. Whatever the silvery thing had been, it was hidden now. "Guys!" he said, pointing. "Did you see that?"

"See what?" Grady asked, looking where Max pointed.

"I didn't see anything," Allie said.

"It was silver," Max said. "And it was moving fast. I don't see it now. We'd better be careful."

"It's hard to be careful in a place like this," Allie said.

"All the more reason to be on our guard," Max said. "I've got a feeling—" He paused. "I feel like the Enemy is spying on us. I think he *wants* us to think we're safe. That's when he'll pounce on us."

"Hey, McCrane!" Toby yelled. "Look out!"

Max turned and—

Splat!

A globe of juicy red fruit hit him in the chest, right on

the Hurley logo of his white tee shirt. Sticky pink juice spattered all across the front of the shirt. Max staggered backward and his glasses fell into the dirt.

A few yards away, Toby laughed uproariously.

Allie was furious. "Toby Brubaker, you brat!"

"'You brat! You brat!'" Toby mocked, giggling.

Max bent down and picked up his glasses. "Look at my shirt! And you could have busted my glasses!"

"Toby," Allie said, "you're such a child!"

"'Such a child! Such a child!'" Toby laughed and snorted through his nose.

"Shut up, Brubaker," Grady said. "Nobody thinks you're funny."

Toby made a face. "You dorks just don't have a sense of humor." He viciously yanked another piece of fruit off a tree. "Besides," he said, "this fruit is *nasty*. I want *real* food—a burger and fries, not this garbage." He hurled the fruit at a tree trunk, where it splattered. Some of the juice sprayed on Grady.

"Hey!" Grady shouted, wiping the sticky droplets from his cheek. He chased Toby, but Toby took refuge behind a tree, dodging back and forth, cackling insanely. Angry as he was, Grady just couldn't get at him—so he gave up. "Just stay out of my way, Brubaker," he warned, "or I'll bust you up—Enemy or no Enemy."

"Come on, Grady," Max said. "Let's find that stream. You and I *both* need to wash up."

Max, Grady, and Allie walked out of the shade of the grove and down the slope. Allie checked over her shoulder to make sure Toby was following them. At the bottom of the slope, they found a series of little waterfalls that tumbled down moss-covered ledges into a shady stream. Max and Grady knelt side by side at the stream and splashed water on themselves, washing themselves the best they could. The water was cool and refreshing to drink.

"Max! Grady!" Allie whispered, standing on a rock beside the stream. "Look!"

The boys looked where Allie pointed. A white-tailed deer with a reddish brown coat was on the opposite side of the stream, next to a large boulder. As they watched, the deer bent its head to drink from the stream.

Splat! A big splotch of red and pink fruit exploded against the boulder. Some of it splashed on the deer. It looked startled and backed away from the fruit-splotch, blinking the juice from its large brown eyes. But it wasn't afraid.

Allie whirled and saw Toby up the hill, a nasty grin on his face. He held another piece of fruit in his hands and was preparing to throw again.

"Toby! No!" she yelled.

Toby hurled the fruit. It sailed in a high arc and landed in the stream, splashing water up on the stream bank—but it missed the deer by a good three feet. The deer looked at Toby with a curious expression, then turned, put its white tail in the air, and casually walked away.

Enraged, Grady scrambled up the hill toward Toby.

Smirking, Toby backed away toward the shade of the grove.

"Get out of here, Brubaker!" Grady yelled. "Just get lost!"

"No! Wait!" Allie called. "Toby, come down here with us! We don't know where the Enemy is or when he'll show up! We've got to stay together!"

"Dude!" Toby chuckled. "Like I want to hang out with a bunch of losers! I'm bored. I'm going to find something fun to do." He walked away, moving along the edge of the trees.

"Let him go," Grady said. "We're better off without him."

"You're wrong," Allie said. "I know Toby's been nothing but trouble, but we still need each other. I don't know what the Enemy intends to do to us, but I know we can't beat him if we're divided against each other."

Max trudged up the hill to join Grady and Allie. His shirt was soaked from his attempt to clean it—but the pink stains were still there. "Maybe I should go after Toby," Max offered.

"No," Grady said. "If the three of us get split-up, we're really sunk. Toby knows where to find us."

Allie glanced worriedly at the top of the hill as Toby disappeared over the rise. "I just hope he comes back," she said, "before the Enemy shows up."

Toby trudged up the grassy hill in a foul mood. Occasionally, he saw a bird on a tree limb or a squirrel on the ground, and he would pick up a rock and try out his aim. Fortunately for the animals in Eden, Toby's aim wasn't very good.

"This whole trip is whack, man!" he grumbled out loud. "It's all McCrane's fault—him and his dorky Timebender! And Grady Stubblefield, the big man, always bossing people around! And Miss Holier-Than-Everybody Allie O'Dell! She's always like, 'Let's pray about it! Let's pray about it!' How lame is that? What is she, some kind of saint? And that Gavriyel, Mister Glow-in-the-Dark Tough Dude! Too big a coward to do his own dirty work, he has to send a bunch of kids to do it for him! That's totally messed up, man! That is so—*Oooof!*"

Toby tripped and went flying. For a few moments, he lay sprawled on Eden's grassy carpet. Then he clambered to his feet, using every swear word in his vocabulary. He looked down—

And saw a glint of silver in the grass!

He had tripped over something stretched across the ground, half-hidden by the tall grass. He bent down for a closer look, carefully parting the grass, and saw—

Something long, shiny, and mirror-polished. It seemed to be made of pure sterling silver, but intricately detailed, with perfectly formed scales, like the scales of a snake. Each scale was a shiny little mirror that reflected Toby's pudgy face in miniature. Whatever this silvery thing in the grass might be, it was shaped like a snake. It was long and curving, and it trailed through the grass and up the hill.

Toby followed the silver thing to see how long it was and where it led. And as he followed it, he found that it was encrusted here and there with glittering white diamonds, red rubies, green emeralds, and blue sapphires. It snaked around rocks and under bushes, leading right into a cave at the edge of a grassy clearing.

Reaching the cave, Toby parted the vines at the opening with his hands—and almost jumped out of his skin!

Toby stared into a huge reptilian face, like the face of a snake made of polished silver, with eyes of red fire. The pupils in the eyes were vertical slits of darkness, like the depths of a bottomless well. Twin curls of black smoke rose from its nostrils. A forked tongue flicked out between gleaming silvery fangs.

Toby Brubaker was face-to-face with the Dragon of Eden.

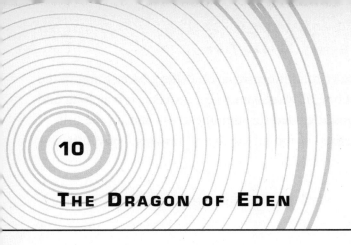

10

THE DRAGON OF EDEN

Allie looked worried. "How long has Toby been gone?" she asked.

Max checked his watch. "Twenty minutes—maybe more."

Allie looked at the ground beside the stream, noticing the trampled grass. "Let's go find him," she said. "The way the grass smashes under our feet, it shouldn't be hard to follow his trail."

Grady sat by the stream with a sour expression. He picked up a rock and tossed it into the rushing water— *sploink!* "It's okay with me if Toby *stays* lost," he said.

"Me, too," Max said, checking the pink spatters across the Hurley logo of his shirt. "The creep ruined my shirt. It was brand-new."

"Come on," Allie said. "We need to find Toby before the Enemy does."

Max frowned. Allie was right. "Okay," he said with an exaggerated sigh. "Let's go find him."

Grady nodded grimly, then got to his feet.

They started climbing the hill, following Toby's tracks.

Twin puffs of smoke blew from the nostrils of the Silver Dragon.

Toby yelped and stumbled backward from the mouth of the cave, falling into a clump of flowering gorse. He was so frightened, he didn't even notice the spiny gorse prickles that poked him in the back. "Please don't kill me!" he blubbered.

"Kill you!" the Dragon said with a roar of laughter. "You've nothing to be afraid of here! I was *expecting* you."

"Expecting . . . me?"

"Of course! I have been watching you since you came to the Garden—you and your friends." Flames licked the Dragon's lips.

"My friends?" With a painful expression, Toby raised himself off the gorse prickles and got to his feet. "Those losers? They're no friends of mine!"

The Dragon smiled—and a charming, likable smile it was. "They've been unkind to you, have they?"

"Bunch of dorks," Toby said.

"Yes," the Dragon said, his voice dripping with sympathy.

"I see that now. A bunch of, um, dorks. They treat you unfairly, accuse you of all sorts of things, spoil your fun, that sort of thing."

"You don't know the half of it."

"They dragged you on this harebrained adventure, and nearly got you killed."

"You got that right."

"We shall have to do something about them," the Dragon said. "They need to be taught a lesson." The Dragon uncoiled himself from the tight confines of the cave. Emerging into the sunlight, he displayed his impressive size. He had four legs and a pair of folded wings—all mirror-finished in silver and overlaid with gemstones. "Well, I am just the one to teach them that lesson. They will treat you a lot differently once they see you have a dragon for a friend." He bent his foreleg and lowered his head in a deep bow. "My name is Lux."

"Cool!" Toby said. "You really want to be my friend? Awesome! But why do you want to be friends with me? You don't know me. You don't even know my name."

"I have looked into your mind . . . Toby," Lux said.

Toby's eyes widened. "Dude!"

"I know where you've come from," Lux continued, "and I know what you want: power to rule over your friends, power to punish your enemies. And, Toby, I can give you that power—*if* you will follow me. A dragon can be a powerful friend to have. I would always be there to serve you and do anything you ask."

"Anything?"

"Anything at all."

"Like, if I wanted to win the grand prize at Invention Convention—you could fix it for me?"

The Dragon paused to scan Toby's mind, then chuckled. "A simple matter," he said. "And as you grow older, and your dreams grow bigger, I will be with you, helping to make all your dreams come true."

The Dragon made a sweeping gesture with his foreleg. Instantly, Toby's mind flooded with an image of himself as a great world leader. He stood in a city plaza, surrounded by marble columns. There was a tall, bronze statue of him towering over the plaza—and since Toby couldn't imagine what he would look like as a man, it was a statue of a cruel-looking boy with a butch haircut, pug nose, little eyes, and an arrogant sneer. Thousands of people thronged the plaza, cheering him, calling, "Toby! Toby! Toby!" He was the Big Boss. If anyone opposed him, made fun of him, or called him names, Toby could have him punished on the spot. And dude! He had some really *cool* punishments planned for the people he hated!

The Dragon knew what was in Toby's heart. He knew that hate was Toby's friend; hurting other people made Toby feel big. The Dragon fed him visions of power, visions of fame—but above all, visions of getting even with everyone!

"Your life can be so wonderful, Toby," the Dragon said, "with me as your friend."

"What do I have to do?" Toby asked.

"Just one little thing," Lux said. "Simply let me make an invisible mark on your forehead—a mark that only I can see."

Toby frowned. He wasn't sure he liked that idea. "Why do you need to make a mark on me?"

"Oh, it won't hurt," Lux said. "I only want to place my seal upon you. No one else will see it. It will be our secret."

Toby thought about it. "And the dream you showed me—you'll make it happen? You promise?"

"Trust me," Lux said. "My power will always be there to serve you."

"Even at Invention Convention?"

The Dragon laughed. "Of course. The grand prize is yours."

Toby grinned. "I'll fix that Max McCrane—him and his stupid Timebender! Okay, Lux, I'm ready. Put the mark on me!"

Silver Dragon reached out with his three-clawed forefoot. The longest of the three claws touched Toby's forehead. A brilliant spark of light, like an electric arc, leaped from the claw to Toby's head. Toby shrieked and fell backward into the grass.

He was as still as death.

Max, Allie, and Grady were walking along a grassy ridge, following Toby's tracks. "If the Enemy is going to show himself," Max said, "I wish he'd end the suspense and—"

That's when they heard Toby shriek.

"Toby!" Allie called.

"Come on!" Grady yelled as he took off running, with Max and Allie close behind. They followed the trampled grass up the hill toward a rocky place surrounded by shrubs and trees. They plunged through a stand of fragrant lilacs and stumbled into a clearing in front of a cave.

Their eyes fell on Toby, stretched out on the grass. Standing over Toby was the last thing they expected to see—a great silver dragon. The Dragon smiled at Max, Allie, and Grady as if he were expecting them. A gust of smoke puffed from his nostrils.

Allie seemed paralyzed. She couldn't take her eyes off the Dragon.

"Don't worry about your friend," the silver-skinned beast said. "He hasn't been harmed."

Toby's eyes blinked open.

"Toby?" Max said. "Are you okay?"

Toby sat up and looked at Max, Allie, and Grady. He was grinning—and it was not a friendly grin. "What's up, guys?" he said, a strange look in his eyes. He glanced up at the Dragon, who towered over him. "I see you met my friend, Lux."

"Your friend?" Grady said. "Your friend's a . . . a *dragon!*"

"Yeah," Toby said. "Pretty cool, huh?"

Max tried to take a step backward, but he was so scared, his knees felt like Jell-O.

But Allie wasn't scared at all. Instead, her eyes were wide with joy. "A dragon!" she said in a hushed whisper. "A *real* dragon! Oh, Max, he's so beautiful! He looks like Sarpane in *The Silver Serpent of Argenna*. Only he's even bigger and more beautiful than J. Farthington Frimby could have imagined!"

"But dragons are dangerous, Allie!" Max whispered. "More dangerous than a tyrannosaur, even!"

"Yeah!" Grady said. "Don't dragons, like, breathe fire and eat people?"

"Well," Allie said, "in the books I've read, there are good dragons and bad dragons. But the good dragons are always beautiful like this one."

"Of course he's a good dragon," Toby said. "His name is Lux, and he can look inside your head and read your thoughts."

"There's something wrong here," Max said. "Gavriyel never said anything about meeting a dragon."

Lux grinned broadly, and flames danced in his mouth. "Gavriyel!" he said brightly. "You know my old friend Gavriyel? When you see him again, tell him that Lux sends his *warmest* greetings!"

"You see, Max?" Allie said. "Lux and Gavriyel are friends. So stop worrying. When the Enemy shows up, Lux can protect us from him."

"Of course I can," the Dragon snorted with pride. "Whoever this Enemy is, I will surely protect you. No harm will come to you as long as I am here. Now—tell me about this Enemy you speak of. What is he like?"

"We only saw him once," Max said, "when we were on Mars."

"Mars?" the Dragon asked.

"The fourth planet from the sun."

"Ah."

"We couldn't see him very well," Allie said, "because he was across the canyon, and it was dark, and there was smoke all around. But I remember he seemed twisted and shadowy, with red, glowing eyes."

"This Enemy sounds absolutely dreadful," the Dragon said. "Like something out of a nightmare."

"Worse than any nightmare I ever had," Allie said. "Lux, I've read lots of books about dragons. I always thought stories about dragons were nothing but fantasy. But now—"

"Yes," Lux said. "Now you know the stories are true! My dear, it is a pleasure to meet an admirer of my species. Come over here, by my cave, young friends. Sit beside me and I will tell you *true* stories of dragonkind."

So Allie sat down by the mouth of the cave, and Lux lay down on the grass, half-encircling her with his long neck and even longer tail. Allie snuggled against the Dragon, stroking his silvery skin and listening to the beating of his nine enormous hearts. Max, Grady, and Toby sat down on the grass in front of the Dragon, and he raised one silvery wing to shield them from the heat of the sun. As they listened, Lux told them tale after enchanting tale.

Lux told them of Zorameth, a sea-dragon who survived many battles against warriors and dragon-hunters, but died of a broken heart when her husband, Yeoboth, was captured, dragged onto the land, and killed. He told them of the Dragon of al-Khem, who could change at will from dragon to human form—and who died tragically when he was captured, put in chains, and cruelly prevented from returning to his dragon shape. He told them of Leviathan, greatest of all dragons, whose back is like a row of shields and whose eyes are as bright as the rising sun, and who now sleeps at the bottom of the sea, never to awaken until the end of the world. In his stories, dragons were never evil or cruel. They were either the characters you admired and cheered for, or the characters you felt sorry for.

After listening to a few stories, Grady got up and walked away from the group. He leaned against a stately yew tree and looked off into the sky, thinking his own private thoughts.

The Dragon watched Grady closely. When he had finished telling of the tragic quest of the Wyrmling Ereoth, Lux said, "Your friend seems to have lost interest in my stories."

"Your stories are wonderful," Allie said. "But Grady has been through a terrible tragedy of his own."

"I know all about Grady's father," Lux said. "I think I can help. Excuse me, friends—I'm going to go talk to him." The Dragon raised himself from the grass, uncoiled his body from around Allie, and walked over to Grady's side.

Grady felt the Dragon's warm breath on his neck. He looked at Lux, and his eyes were sad. "If it's okay with you," Grady said, "I'd like to be alone right now."

"If you wish," the Dragon said in a soft, sympathetic voice. "I know about the loss of your father. I, too, understand grief." A luminous tear formed in the corner of the Dragon's eye. "This God you trusted has let you down," Lux said. "Not much of a friend, I say. No wonder you don't believe in Him anymore. But don't worry, Grady, I am your *true* friend. I will never let you down." The Dragon's voice was soothing and gentle. "You trust me, don't you?"

Grady looked the Dragon in the eye. "Can you help me see my dad again?"

The Dragon sighed deeply. "There are some things even a dragon can't do. But there are other ways I can help you. I can be a friend throughout your life. I know you want to be a great athlete someday. Just name the sport—football, baseball, basketball, any sport you choose. I'll make you a star, a real Hall of Famer."

Images flooded Grady's mind. He saw himself raising the Lombardi Trophy at the Super Bowl . . . and hitting his hundredth home run of the season as cheers and fireworks went up around the baseball stadium . . . and streaking in the open court and swooping under the basket for a dazzling reverse lay-up, clinching the NBA Finals.

"You'll be rich beyond belief," the Dragon said as the vision faded from Grady's mind. "You'll have fans by the millions. You'll be a legend."

"What do I have to do?" Grady asked.

"Do?" the Dragon replied. "Just a small thing. Practically nothing at all. Simply receive my mark on your forehead, and I'll be your friend for life. Think it over, Grady. Your future can be anything you desire—*if* you have a dragon for a friend."

Leaving Grady to his dreams of the future, the Dragon walked over to Allie. She was standing in the middle of the grassy clearing, a look of concern on her face. "Is Grady okay?" she asked.

"He'll be fine," Lux said. He glanced over by the mouth of the cave, where Max and Toby were arguing. "What's going on between those two?" he asked.

Allie rolled her eyes. "Boys! They're so immature! Max is mad at Toby for ruining his shirt, and Toby is bragging to Max that his Invention Convention project will win the grand prize. I've had it with both of them!"

The Dragon laughed. "I understand your frustration, Allie," he said. "It must be annoying to have to put up with such a pair of, um, children."

"Exactly!" Allie said. "They're acting like children, both of them!"

"The moment I saw you," the Dragon continued, "I said to myself, 'Now, there's a young lady with grown-up ideas! She has a tremendous future ahead of her.'"

Allie smiled shyly, and her braces flashed in the sunlight. "Really?"

"In fact," Lux added, "I can see your entire future right now."

Allie gasped. "Really? Tell me! No, wait! Don't tell me! I don't want to know! . . . No, wait! Tell me! I've got to know! . . . No, wait!—Oh, I don't know if I want to know or not!"

Lux chuckled. "Your future," he said, "is whatever you want it to be—if you'll accept my help." The Dragon's eyes had a soothing, almost hypnotic effect on Allie.

"Accept your help?" Allie asked, puzzled. "What do you mean?"

"I know what your dream is. You stand on a stage in a sparkling formal gown, your eyes shining like diamonds in the spotlight."

Listening to the Dragon, Allie could see it, too. She closed her eyes as he continued. His voice was strangely persuasive, and it filled her mind with images so real, she could practically reach out and touch them.

"You hold a golden statue in your hands," the Dragon said, "and you are so thrilled you can hardly speak. The applause of the audience is deafening. A dozen TV cameras are focused on you. The whole world is watching as you open your mouth to say—"

"I'd like to thank the Academy—," Allie said, her eyes closed, her face wearing a dreamy smile. Suddenly, she stopped, and her eyes popped open. "An Academy Award? For me? Is that really my future?"

"That future is yours," Lux said, "if you want it. Fame. Applause. Your face on thousands of movie screens. Millions of adoring fans. All you have to do is receive my mark—and I'll be your friend forever."

"A dragon for a friend!" Allie said, her eyes shining. "I feel like I'm living in a novel—"

Just then, Max came stamping over, a scowl on his face. "That Toby Brubaker is such a jerk!" he growled. "He says he's going to rule the world, and everybody's going to bow down to him, and he's going to get even with me for dragging him away from his own time! I never met anyone so full of himself!"

"I wouldn't worry about Toby," Allie said. "He's always acting bigger than he is."

"I don't know," Max said. "The way he's talking is really scary."

"There's nothing wrong with a boy having ambition," the Dragon said. "After all, Max, I'm sure you have ambitions of your own, *don't you?*"

"Ambitions?" Max said. "No, I don't think so—"

"Excuse us, won't you, Allie?" said the Dragon, placing one silvery wing around Max's shoulder and guiding him away.

"Sure," Allie said.

The Dragon led Max to the edge of the clearing. "Max, my boy, I recognized it the moment I saw you. You have wonderful, noble ambitions! Not a crude, selfish craving for power and glory, like that jerk Toby Brubaker. No, Max, you have brains! You dream of becoming a great scientist, a great inventor. And I shall see to it that you receive a truly fitting honor for your brilliance—the Nobel Prize!"

Max's eyes lit up. "Me? Win the Nobel Prize? I mean— you really think I could?"

"Max," Lux said, leaning his face so close that the boy could feel the furnace-heat of his breath, "I guarantee it. In fact, you'll be the youngest Nobel winner in history. And do you know why?"

Max slowly shook his head. "Why?"

Lux spoke one word: "Timebender."

Max's eyes went wide. "Timebender!"

"Max! It's the most amazing invention in human history— and *you* invented it! And when you get back to your own time, I'll be there—invisible but right alongside you, guiding you every step of the way. They'll fly you to Stockholm, and the king of Sweden will bestow the Nobel medal on you, and the entire world will applaud the boy genius!"

Instantly, Max had a vision of himself on the stage, receiving the applause of the crowd. He saw the proud faces of his mom and dad as they stood next to him. He saw the king of Sweden, and he felt the golden weight of the medal as it was hung around his neck: Max McCrane, youngest Nobel winner in history!

"You like that future, don't you, Max?" the Dragon asked.

The vision was fading, but it left a strange feeling inside Max. It was a sneaking sense of "I'm-so-smart" and "I'm-so-great" and "I'm-so-superior-to-everyone-else." This was a totally new experience for Max, because he had never been a stuck-up sort of person at all. He had never wanted to be better than anyone else, and he had never looked down on anyone else. But there was something about the vision the Dragon had put in his mind. It made him not only *think* he was better and more important than other people, but it made him *enjoy* that nasty feeling of superiority.

Max blinked at the Dragon. "Is it really true?" he asked. "Is all of that really going to happen to me?"

"It's true," the Dragon answered slyly, "if you want it to be. Just receive my mark, and it will all happen—and a lot more besides."

Max didn't even have to think about it. The answer was yes.

Max, Allie, and Grady stood in a line in front of the cave, ready to receive the mark of the Dragon—and Toby Brubaker didn't like it one bit. He took Lux aside and hissed, "No fair!

You said you'd help me get even with those dorks! Teach them a lesson, you said! Now you're going to give them the same mark you gave me!"

"Easy, Toby, easy!" the Dragon said in a soothing voice, speaking softly so the others would not hear. "You're my *real* friend, Toby. This is all part of the plan. I'm just *pretending* to be friends with those, um, dorks. Once they've received my mark, they will be my slaves. But *you* are the one I will give the *real* power to, Toby. Just wait until you see the nasty surprises I have planned for those three!"

"Oh, I get it!" A grin spread across Toby's face. "Cool!"

With a swish of its long, glittering tail, the Dragon whirled about and faced the three young time travelers. "My friends," he said, "it's time!"

Max, Allie, and Grady glanced at each other. "I'm ready," Max said.

"We're all ready," Allie said.

"Excellent," Lux chuckled. He raised his left foreclaw toward Max's head. "From this day forward, you will be my friends, my followers. You will call to me, and I will come. You will pray to me, and I will answer."

The silver claw reached for Max's brow. Max closed his eyes, smiling.

"Wait!" Allie said.

Max jerked his head back. The claw had been within a quarter-inch of his skin. "What is it, Allie?" he asked.

The Dragon exhaled a black puff of annoyance. "Yes," he said. "What is it, Allie?"

Allie shook her head as if to clear the cobwebs from her mind. "That's not right—"

Max's mind felt cloudy and sluggish as if he were waking from a dream. "What's not right?"

Allie grabbed Max by the sleeve and pulled him away from the Dragon. "Max," she said, "you don't *pray* to a dragon. You pray to *God*."

"Allie . . . ," Lux said. His tone was soft, yet threatening—like an iron fist in a velvet glove.

Allie turned to face the Dragon. "Lux—a while ago, you said, 'When you see my *old friend* Gavriyel'—You know what, Mr. Dragon? The last time we saw the Enemy, he called Gavriyel 'old friend,' too."

"Allie," Max said, "are you saying that Lux is—"

"That's exactly what I'm saying," Allie said. "Lux *is* the Enemy."

The Dragon scowled and paced back and forth. "You wound me deeply," he said—but his voice didn't sound sad. It sounded *furious*.

"Remember what Gavriyel told us: 'The Enemy is a deceiver. He can assume many pleasing shapes,'" Allie said.

The Dragon looked at Max and Grady. "Your friend Allie is being very foolish," he growled. "When the *real* Enemy comes, I won't be able to protect her. You must believe in me, or I cannot help you."

Grady stepped forward, eyes shining. "I believe in you!" he said.

The Dragon smiled at Grady and said, "A wise young man." He turned to Max and lifted his claw toward Max's brow. "And you, Max? You believe in me, don't you?"

There was a look of confusion in Max's eyes. "I—I don't know what to believe."

"Max," Allie said, "you saw the silver thing moving through the trees in the Garden. Max! It was Lux. He was watching us."

"I am not your enemy," said the Dragon, stamping his foot. Angry black plumes puffed from his nostrils. "I am your friend!"

Max took a step toward the Dragon—but Allie pulled him away. "No, Max! Don't go near him!"

The Dragon whirled on Allie, eyes glaring, mouth and nostrils aflame. "Perhaps you have heard the saying: Do not meddle in the affairs of dragons, for you are crunchy and taste good with ketchup!"

"I know that saying," Allie said. "It's from *White Unicorn, Black Dragon.* I've read that book a dozen times—as I'm sure you know, since you can read my mind. But at the beginning of that book, J. Farthington Frimby quotes from the last book of the Bible, and I've read that quote so many times I have it memorized."

"No!" snarled the Dragon. "Shut up!"

"It goes like this: 'And there was a war in heaven.

Michael and his angels fought against the dragon—and the dragon and his angels fought back. But he was not strong enough, and they lost their place in heaven. The great dragon was cast out—'"

"You—," the Dragon said. "You *wicked* girl!"

"I know what those words mean now," Allie said.

"Yeah," Max said, looking at the Dragon as if seeing him for the very first time. "I do, too! Allie, we saw that war with our own eyes! We saw the Dragon thrown down to the earth!"

"Max!" the Dragon said. "Don't let her turn you against me!"

But what the Dragon feared had already come to pass. The eyes of Max's soul were opened. All the nasty, stuck-up feelings that had seemed so pleasurable a moment before—the feeling of "I'm-so-smart" and "I'm-so-great" and "I'm-so-superior-to-everyone-else"—now just seemed ridiculous. Suddenly, Max realized where that nasty feeling of self-importance came from. It was the same self-important feeling the Enemy felt when he rebelled against Elyon. It was that nasty feeling of superiority that had turned Lightbringer into the Devil.

"He fooled us, Allie," Max said.

"And I know *how* he fooled us, Max," Allie said. "When we first arrived here, I was thinking how beautiful this place is, and how it reminded me of the beautiful Dragon Lands in the Frimby books. Lux was there in the woods, spying on us, reading my thoughts. He looked inside my mind, saw how much I love dragons, and he knew that if he appeared as a shining dragon, I would be fooled! And it worked—for a while."

Max's eyes widened. "Yeah! He fooled me so completely that I didn't even notice the Dragon's *name*. Allie, 'Lux' is a scientific term—it comes from the Latin word for light! The Enemy is Lux—Lightbringer! This is the test Gavriyel warned us about—and we almost failed it!"

The Dragon reared his head and roared, expelling great orange billows of flame. Allie screamed and pulled Max away from the Dragon, toward the edge of the clearing.

On the far side of the clearing, Toby laughed at their fear. "Show them, Lux! Show those dorks what power really is!"

Standing by the cave, just a few feet from the Dragon, Grady looked skyward, watching the cloud of flame and smoke rise above him. The Dragon's long, silvery neck curved over Grady, and its snakelike eyes peered into his with hypnotic power. "Grady," the Dragon said, "your two friends have turned against me. But you won't forsake me, will you? Receive my mark, and you'll have wealth, fame, and power beyond your wildest dreams!" The Dragon raised his foreclaw to Grady's brow.

Grady looked steadily at the claw, smiling and nodding. "I'm ready," he said.

"Grady! Listen to me!"

Grady snapped his head around and saw Allie approaching. She stretched out her hand. "Don't give in to the Enemy!"

Grady backed away from her. "He may be *your* enemy, but he's *my* friend," he snarled. "The Dragon showed me the future, Allie—*my* future! I *want* that future!" He took a step toward the Dragon's outstretched claw.

"Grady, wait!" Max shouted, running up alongside Allie. "Before Gavriyel left us here, Allie and I prayed to be protected from the Enemy. God heard our prayer."

"So," said Grady, "God answered your prayer?"

Allie's eyes shone with tears. "Yes, Grady," she said. "He really did."

Grady's face turned hard, and his voice was bitter. "Well, isn't that nice?" he said. "I wonder why He hears your prayers—and ignores mine? I prayed, too, remember? When my dad was dying, I prayed every day, and what did God do? Nothing! He let my father die!"

Allie's face sagged, and tears spilled down her cheeks. "Grady, please—"

"You know who cares about me?" Grady said. "The Dragon! He's the only *real* friend I have." He turned and raised his forehead to the Dragon's claw. "I'm ready, Lux! Put your mark on me!"

The Dragon grinned triumphantly. The glittering claw moved toward Grady's brow.

On the far side of the clearing, Toby chuckled.

There was no time to think. Max and Allie leaped into

action. Allie jumped straight at Grady, putting a football-style tackle on him and knocking him to the ground. Max leaped for the Dragon's claw, slapping it away from Grady's face. The Dragon gave a grunt of surprise and swung the clawed foot backward, cuffing Max in the mouth and knocking him off his feet. Max fell to the grass with a bloody lip.

The Dragon reared up over Max. "Stay out of this, boy," Lux snarled. "Your friend has made his choice! He belongs to me!"

Behind the Dragon, Grady climbed to his feet. Allie jumped up and threw herself at the back of his knees—another flying football tackle. Grady went facedown onto the grass as the Dragon's silvery tail lashed mere inches over his head.

"Stay down!" Allie shouted, trying to hold Grady on the ground.

The hot blast of the Dragon's breath washed over Max's face. He scrambled across the grass under the angry eyes of the Dragon. "Grady doesn't understand you like we do," Max shouted, straightening his glasses. "But Allie and I know *who* you are and *what* you are—and we won't let you have him!"

The Dragon answered with a bone-shaking roar and a blast of crackling, white-hot flame. The heat from the fire caused Max to break out in a fevered sweat. "Don't interfere," Lux roared, "or you'll be destroyed!"

Toby dashed forward and threw himself at Max, slamming into him like a freight train. Blindsided, Max was knocked face-first onto the ground. The impact sent his glasses flying and opened a bloody gash in his cheek.

Behind the Dragon, Grady struggled out of Allie's grasp and rose to his feet. "Lux!" he shouted. "I'm ready! Put your mark on me!"

The Dragon whirled, tail lashing.

Allie struggled to her feet, reaching for Grady, but she stumbled over a stone—fortunately for her. As she went sprawling in the grass, the Dragon's tail whip-cracked the air over her head, missing her by inches. But the Dragon's tail didn't miss Grady. It struck him squarely in the chest with tremendous force. Grady sailed across the clearing and landed with a sickening *smack!* against a tree trunk.

Allie raised her head and saw Grady's body flop onto the grass at the base of the tree. He seemed as lifeless as a rag doll. Allie screamed.

A few yards away, on the other side of the Dragon, Toby scrambled to his feet and prepared to launch himself at Max again. Then he heard Allie's scream, and his head whipped around—and he saw Grady's lifeless body by the tree.

Max groped in the grass, searching for his glasses. He found them at the same moment he heard Allie scream. He jumped to his feet, slid the glasses onto his face—and saw Grady's body lying askew on the grass. "Oh, no!" he groaned.

Max dashed toward Grady, heedless of the danger of running right under the fire-spitting nostrils of an enraged dragon. He arrived at Grady's side seconds after Allie.

As Allie cradled Grady's head, Max gently turned his body over. Blood oozed from a gash in front of Grady's left ear. His eyes were closed.

He was not breathing.

Holding Grady's head in her lap, Allie cried bitterly.

"Oh, God!" Max prayed. "Don't let him die!"

Toby came running toward them, but stopped a few yards away, staring. The Dragon came up behind Toby, spouting vile puffs of black smoke.

"You fixed him, Lux!" Toby sneered. "You fixed him good!"

The Dragon cuffed Toby with his silvery wing. "Ow!" Toby whined.

"Fool!" the Dragon growled, blowing a furious billow of smoke. "The boy is no use to me dead!"

11

THE VOICE IN THE WOODS

The next thing Grady knew, he was in another place. He stood up, remembering a horrible impact and a flash of pain—but when he felt his head and checked himself over, he found that he was not hurt at all. He felt fine, absolutely fine.

He remembered where he had come from. He remembered a dragon and a cave. He remembered friends.

Odd, he hadn't thought of them as friends before, but they had risked their lives to save him from the Dragon— to keep him from destroying his own soul. Only friends would do that. He never even got a chance to thank his friends.

The air was filled with a peaceful, golden light. He was standing on a smooth path that led across a green and grassy countryside. There were tranquil woods on either side of the path, and overhead was a dome of dazzling blue sky and cotton-candy clouds. Everywhere Grady looked, the colors were the most intense he had ever seen.

The pathway he stood upon was paved with smooth, flat stones of polished gold. It led to a distant city, the spires of which seemed to be made of diamonds and other precious stones. As he looked toward the beautiful city, he felt an aching longing to go there.

Grady began walking toward the city.

He had only taken a dozen steps when he saw the man. Grady's footsteps slowed—then stopped. The man was far away, coming out of the city, walking straight toward Grady on the golden road. He was only a vague outline against the bright glare of the city spires. Even so, Grady instantly recognized him.

"Dad!" he shouted. "Dad!"

Grady ran straight up the path toward the man from the city. Soon, the man was running, too. They rushed together and embraced each other.

"It's okay, son," his father said. "Everything's okay now."

"Dad," Grady said, tears rolling freely down his face. "I thought I'd never see you again! This isn't a dream, is it?"

"No, son." His father laughed—that rich and wonderful laugh that Grady remembered so well. "This is no dream. This is as real as it gets!"

Grady looked around him. What his father said was true. There was nothing dreamlike about these surroundings, about the clear, rich detail of the grass and the trees and the golden road. Most of all, there was nothing dreamlike about his father. He no longer looked gaunt and weak, as he had during Grady's last visit to the hospital. Incredibly, he looked strong and healthy, with a glad, hearty face and bands of powerful muscles rippling beneath the even, black skin of his arms. Grady could still feel the hug his dad had given him—firm and forceful, a rib-squeezer of a hug.

No, this was not a dream. This was definitely real.

"Dad," Grady said, "I've been trying to get back to you."

"I know, Grady," his dad said. "I tried to tell you when I was leaving, after I died. You were walking home. I tried to tell you everything was okay."

"I heard you," Grady said, "but I didn't believe it."

Grady's father put his arm around the boy's shoulders. Grady slipped his arm around his dad. Together, they began walking toward the shining city.

"I know it must have hurt you terribly when I left," his father said. "You don't know how much I wanted to stay. But you haven't been alone."

That's when Grady noticed the light. The peaceful golden light. It seemed to be everywhere, yet it seemed to come from nowhere. There was no sun in the sky. The light simply shone upon the grass and the trees and the golden path. It flowed like honey in the air all around them. It shone from the city in front of them. The light was everywhere, and there were no shadows anywhere. The light was alive and radiant with love.

"I thought it was just light," Grady said. "But it's Him, isn't it?"

"Yes," his father answered, smiling. "And He has always been with you, even when you were angry with Him."

Grady remembered the bitterness he had felt, and there was a twinge of regret in his chest. But in the next instant, he felt the warmth of the golden light shining on his face. Grady knew he was forgiven.

He held out his hand, and the golden light flowed over his skin—and he realized this was the same golden light that poured from the faces of Gavriyel and the other Emissaries. It was the light of Elyon Himself—and it bubbled up like a spring of sparkling golden water inside everyone in whom Elyon lived. Looking closely, he realized this same golden light danced in his father's eyes and vibrated in his father's voice.

And then Grady remembered the Enemy and the Dark Emissaries. They had once lived in this golden light, but they had rebelled. The golden light was gone from the Dark Emissaries, leaving only a red glare of hate and evil.

Grady and his dad walked the golden pathway for a while in silence, their arms around each other. The city was closer now. Grady could make out more detail in its shining towers. His heart beat faster as he thought of a whole city filled with people who had the golden light shining from their eyes and their souls. He couldn't wait to reach that city—

His father stopped. Grady paused, looking up at his dad. "Why are we stopping?"

His father smiled. "Someone wants to talk to you." He pointed toward the woods on the side of the path.

Grady looked. There was a bright golden light shining among the trees, deep in the heart of the woods. It cast rays of soft light that warmed Grady's face. He took a few steps off the path, and the grass under his feet was like a thick carpet, soft and springy.

"Hello, Grady," said a Voice from the woods. The Voice was golden, like the light.

Grady's heart leaped inside him. "Hi," he said. He instantly thought it was a dumb way to greet this golden Voice, but in the next moment, he knew it was okay. Grady glanced back at his dad, and his dad smiled at him.

"You have many questions, Grady," said the Voice from the woods. "Now you are ready for the answers. You once asked My servant Gavriyel why I allow war and suffering. You wanted to know why your father had to get sick and die."

"Yeah. None of that stuff makes sense to me."

"You saw the war in heaven," the Voice said. "You met the Enemy face-to-face. He is the one who brought sin and death into My creation."

"I understand that," Grady said. "But You created the Enemy, didn't You?"

"I did. He was once a glorious creature. But Lightbringer was seduced by his own desire to be great. He said, 'I will raise myself above the stars of Elyon; I will be like the Most High.' It was his choice that brought evil into My creation."

"But You gave him that choice," Grady said. "I don't mean to disrespect You, but—"

"It's a fair question, Grady," said the Voice, in a tone full of kindness and understanding. "Yes, I gave Lightbringer the power to choose good or evil. Every soul, whether human or Emissary, has the power to choose. Free will is a good thing, even though it might be misused. Without the power to choose, you are nothing but a robot. I did not create robots, Grady. I created living *souls.*"

Grady took a few steps closer to the light from the woods. "But that doesn't explain why You let my father die," he said. "I prayed and prayed for You to heal him— but You let him die. I'm not mad at You anymore, but I still don't understand *why* You let that happen."

Grady heard soft footsteps behind him. "I can answer that, son."

Grady turned and searched his father's eyes.

"You prayed and God answered," said Grady's dad. "But like your mother says, sometimes the answer is 'No.'"

"But why can't the answer be 'Yes'?" Grady asked. "If God's all-powerful, why can't He work things out so that people don't have to suffer and die?"

"Son," his father said, "I don't completely understand

God's Eternal Plan. No one can understand it until it is completed. But I do know this: When you hurt, God hurts with you. When you're sad, He's sad with you. He didn't cause the evil and hurt in the world, but He can take that bad stuff and use it to do good things in our lives."

Grady looked troubled. "I don't understand."

"Son, do you remember when the only thing you wanted for your tenth birthday was a weight machine? And it had to be that top-of-the-line Body Crafter Multi-Station Gym with the bench press, leg press, ab cruncher—"

Grady chuckled. "I remember."

"And after I spent a whole day setting it up in the garage, you tried it a few times and said, 'It's too hard! It makes my muscles hurt!' Remember?"

Grady grinned. "You told me if I didn't get out there and use it every day, you'd stop my allowance till it was paid for."

"I would have, too," his father said with a big, deep laugh. "Not because I'm mean, but because I love you. I knew you wanted to be an athlete, and I also knew you'd never make it without the pain and strain of pushing against those weights every day. Making things easy on you would have saved you some pain, but it would have made you scrawny and weak. So I pushed you. I started you out with those little bitty weights, and I watched you work your way up to the big gut-busting weights. And you got a lot of sore muscles and you broke a lot of sweat—but that pain made you strong."

His father's grin faded. His voice became serious. "Life's pain hurts a lot more, but God has figured out a way to take that pain and reshape it into something good, something beautiful. He didn't cause those hurts, but He can use them to help us grow stronger in love, stronger in our trust in Him." His father paused, then added. "You know, your friends did you a big favor, saving you from the Dragon. You need to go back and thank them."

"Go back?" Grady exclaimed. "But I don't want to go back! I want to stay here with you!"

"You can't stay here—not yet," his father said in a gentle voice. "Life is short enough as it is, and you'll be here before you know it. You and I will be together—but when the time is right."

Grady gazed longingly down the golden path, toward the shining city. He wanted to go there more than anything. And he wanted to stay with his dad. He turned and faced the golden light in the woods.

"Please," Grady said. "Let me stay."

"Your friends need you," the golden Voice said. "Your mother needs you. And you have so much more to learn. You can only learn it by living."

Grady's shoulders slumped. He knew his dad was right, and so was the Voice. "Okay," he said. "I'll go back."

"Good," the Voice said. "But before you go, let me give you something."

"What is it?" Grady asked.

"A Name," said the Voice. "When you wake up, speak this Name. Say it again and again, until the danger is past and the Enemy is defeated."

Then the Voice told Grady the Name.

Grady laughed. "I know this Name."

"Of course you do," the Voice said.

"Okay," the boy said. "I'm ready to go."

The father and son hugged each other on the golden path. "Good-bye, Dad," Grady said. There were no tears in his eyes, and there was no sadness in his heart.

"Good-bye, son," his father said.

"Don't forget," the Voice said. "Say the Name."

Grady closed his eyes and said the Name.

The Dragon looked down at Grady's body without pity. "A waste," the silvery beast said. "I could have used a boy like him."

Toby stood at the Dragon's side. He was shivering, though it wasn't cold.

Enraged, Max grabbed a stone and hurled it at the Dragon's face. The stone struck the Dragon between the eyes and bounced harmlessly away. The Dragon barely flinched. "Get out of here!" Max yelled. "Go away!"

"This is your fault, Max," the Dragon said calmly. "Yours, too, Allie. Your friend's blood is on your own hands—not mine. Grady wanted to join me. If you hadn't interfered, none of this would have happened, and your friend would still be—" The Dragon stopped. His reptilian eyes popped wide open with surprise.

Allie looked down at Grady—and held her breath. Grady's lips were moving!

The Dragon took a step backward, fear in his eyes.

Grady was speaking the Name.

It was scarcely a whisper—but the Dragon heard the Name and knew he was defeated. The Dragon screamed and howled, backing away. Flames shot from his nostrils, scorching the grass.

Grady's eyelids slowly opened. He saw the Silver Dragon rearing up, eyes staring madly. Great billows of orange flame and black smoke exploded from the Dragon's mouth and nostrils. Grady said the Name again, louder this time.

The Dragon roared. "Shut up, you," the Dragon shrieked, "or I'll blast you to ashes!"

But Grady only laughed and repeated the Name, louder and louder. Allie joined Grady, saying the Name along with him. Max jumped to his feet and shouted the Name.

The silver beast retreated across the grassy clearing, backing away in terror, withdrawing toward the cave. As it retreated, the Dragon vainly tried to cover its ears with its wings—but it couldn't escape the Name.

Max followed the Dragon across the clearing, saying the Name again and again.

"Stop it, McCrane!" Toby shouted. "Stop saying that! You're scaring him! Leave him alone!"

Half in, half out of the cave, the Dragon opened its jaws, bared its fangs, and sent a withering blast of flame rolling across the clearing toward Max. The flames turned to harmless smoke before they ever reached him. Max felt a wave of heat pass over him—and he laughed. Then he spoke the Name one last time—

And the Dragon turned and disappeared into the cave. Every silver scale, claw, fang, and coil of him—

Gone!

"Max!" Allie called. "There goes Toby! Stop him!"

Toby was running toward the cave. Max chased him to the mouth of the cave and tackled him. Toby got back to his feet and, like a boy possessed, tried to hurl himself into the cave after the Dragon. Again, Max tackled him and knocked him to the ground. Though Toby was an inch taller and forty pounds heavier, Max had no trouble over-powering him. Toby lost the will to fight, and Max took him by the arm and led him away from the cave.

The doughy-faced boy was crying and his nose was bloodied. He didn't look much like a bully anymore.

It didn't take Grady long to recover his strength. Allie made him rest for a few minutes, then Grady insisted on getting up and walking back to the Volkswagen. When the four travelers got back to the place where the battered orange Beetle waited, Gavriyel was already there. He was bathed in a golden glow that came from within.

Max, Allie, and Grady all wore broad smiles as they approached the Emissary, but Toby threw himself down against the car's front bumper, sniveling and sulking.

Gavriyel looked at Toby sadly. "He received the mark," the Emissary said. "That is very unfortunate." He turned to Max, Allie, and Grady. "But you three have passed the test."

"Gavriyel, tell us," Allie said, "what was this all about? Why did Elyon choose us for this test?"

"Yeah," Max said. "We're just kids."

"That is precisely the point," Gavriyel said. "Lightbringer was once the greatest of Elyon's entire legion of Emissaries, the most powerful creature in His kingdom. But Lightbringer was seduced by his own greatness. He rebelled against the Most High—that was the great and terrible war you saw. Because of Lightbringer's rebellion, Elyon condemned him to the Pit—but Lightbringer complained that Elyon's judgment was unfair.

"'Rebellion is only natural,' Lightbringer said. 'No creature with a free will would ever choose obedience to You. Free will must always revolt against Authority, and glorify the Self.' That was Lightbringer's defense.

"Elyon rejected that defense and He created human beings—small, weak, mortal creatures who never had the advantages Lightbringer had. Unlike the Enemy, humans have never seen Elyon face-to-face. They live a short time—fewer than a hundred years—and then they die. Yet Elyon loved them, blessed them, and is carrying out the Eternal Plan through them. And in spite of their weakness and limitation, some humans choose—*of their own free will*—to trust and obey the Most High. If mere humans can do that, then the Enemy is without excuse.

"And that is why Elyon chose *you* for this test. Not only are you small, weak, mortal humans, but you are young humans, still in your teens. The Enemy tried to exalt himself above the Most High—but he has been shamed by the small, the weak, the foolish. The three of you have destroyed the Enemy's excuses, and you have proved that the judgment of Elyon is just."

"But how did we do that?" Max asked. "The Enemy is a lot smarter and stronger than we are."

"The Enemy is powerful—but not *all*-powerful," Gavriyel said. "He is crafty—but not wise. Every time he thinks he has won a victory, it turns out to be an even greater disaster for his cause. And still he has not learned his lesson.

"Before long, right here in this very Garden, the Enemy will try once more to defeat the Eternal Plan. He will tempt a man and a woman, and they will fall. Lightbringer will think he has won at last—but he will only succeed in setting Elyon's Great Idea in motion. The Enemy will continue to connive and scheme, century after century, until he achieves his ultimate triumph—the death of Elyon's own Son. The Enemy will laugh as the body of the Son is placed in a tomb. The Enemy will not even suspect that, three days later, the tomb will be empty and the Son will be victorious. Ultimately, the Enemy will go down into the Pit, to be forgotten forever."

Max, Allie, and Grady were silent for a few moments. Then Grady pointed to Toby, who sat on the ground in front of the VW. "What about Toby?" Grady asked. "He received the Dragon's mark. Is he—I mean, will he have to—"

"Will Toby share the same fate as the Enemy?" Gavriyel said. "That's his decision to make. His will is as free now as it ever was. If he will simply place his trust in the Most High, he will be forgiven—and the Dragon will lose all claim to his soul."

"Never!" Toby snapped, his pudgy face twisted with rage and hate. "The Dragon is my friend! He's powerful, and you dorks will all be sorry you made him mad! He'll fix you all!"

Grady shook his head. "Get real, Toby. The Dragon's a loser—and so are you, if you keep following him."

"It is Toby's choice to make what he will of his own life—and his own soul," Gavriyel said. "Come, friends. This adventure is over. It's time for you to return home."

"But we can't go home," Max said. "Timebender doesn't work. The batteries are dead."

Gavriyel raised his arms toward the Volkswagen, and a golden light poured from his hands and enveloped the car. The doors opened by themselves. The car seemed alive and welcoming. Gavriyel turned to them and said, "I think you'll find that your machine is good for one final trip home."

Allie clapped and shouted, "Woohoo!"

Max yelled, "Yes!"

Grady laughed and said, "We're going home!"

They piled into Timebender, Max and Allie in front, Grady and a sulking Toby in back.

Allie raised her eyes heavenward. "Thank You!" she said.

"Amen to that," Grady said.

Max rolled down the window and called out, "Gavriyel! Will we see you again?"

The Emissary smiled. "Elyon knows," he said.

A rainbow-colored flash of light burst through the air. Timebender and its passengers vanished from the Garden, leaving only the impression of its four tires in the cool, green grass.

A soft sigh drifted on the breeze, a shimmer of golden light appeared, and then Gavriyel, too, was gone.

12

And the Winner Is . . .

"I hope you kids are hungry," Mrs. McCrane called. She walked into the room with a tray in her hands. "I brought some milk and cookies for—"

She stopped and stared.

The ugly orange Volkswagen—that horrid old car that Max called "Timebender"—was simply *gone*.

But that was impossible. She had seen it there a short time earlier. And it wouldn't fit through the door.

Suddenly, the tray fell to the floor. Cookies flew. Glasses crashed. Milk splashed everywhere.

Mrs. McCrane ran screaming down the hall.

No sooner had she left the room than there was a rain-bow-colored flash of light—and the battered orange VW Beetle was back.

It was even more crunched and battered than when it

left. The rear of the car was splattered with Cretaceous mud. The windshield and side windows were shattered. The roof was crushed and dented.

"We're back!" Max shouted.

"We're back!" Grady and Allie whooped.

"Let me out, you dorks!" Toby snapped.

They scrambled out of the VW and were standing around it when Dr. and Mrs. McCrane ran into the room and skidded to a stop.

Mrs. McCrane's eyes popped wide and her face turned pale. "It's here, then it's not here," she said in a stunned voice, "then it's here again—"

"Mom," Max said, "maybe you'd better sit down."

Max's mom sat down—on the floor. She was so confused, she forgot to make sure there was a chair under her.

Dr. McCrane walked up to the car and ran his fingers over the row of dents along the roof.

"Teeth marks, Dad," Max explained. "Tyrannosaurus rex."

"Ah."

"Late Cretaceous Period, I think."

Dr. McCrane walked around the back of the car. "And this mud—also from the Cretaceous Period?"

"Dad," Max said, "I can explain—"

"Max," Dr. McCrane said, "I thought we agreed you were not to take this car out of the house without permission. From the look of things, I'd say you broke that agreement by, oh, about eighty million years or so."

Max hung his head. "Sorry, Dad."

"And look at you, Max!" Dr. McCrane said. "You're a mess! Where did you get that cut on your cheek?" He gestured toward Grady. "And who is this young man with the dried mud all over him? I remember meeting Sally here, but this young man—"

"That's Grady," Max said. "He's a friend of mine. He got that mud on him when the ankylosaur nearly hit him in the head with its tail."

"Oh, I see," Dr. McCrane said.

"We also went to outer space," Allie chirped, "and back to the beginning of time!"

"And," Grady added, "we went to the Garden of Eden, and—"

Max nudged them both. Allie and Grady clamped their mouths shut.

Toby saw a chance to get Max into even deeper trouble. "I didn't even want to go!" he said. "Max kidnapped me!"

Dr. McCrane's eyebrows lifted at least an inch. "Max, is all this true?"

"Everything Allie and Grady said is true—," Max began.

"Allie?" Dr. McCrane said. "I thought her name was Sally."

"—but Toby's just trying to cause trouble," Max finished. "Go home, Toby."

Toby made a rude noise. Then he turned, went to the open window, climbed out, and left the McCrane House the same way he came in.

"So," Dr. McCrane said sternly, "you really have been traveling all over time and space in this old Volkswagen. You know what that means, don't you?"

Max nodded, shamefaced. "It means you're going to yell at me."

"No," Dr. McCrane said, a grin spreading across his face, "it means this Timebender idea of yours really works! Max! How did you do it? When you said you wanted to build a time machine, I never dreamed—"

"Oswald McCrane!" Mrs. McCrane shouted, seated on the floor. "Help me to my feet!"

"Huh? Oh, yes, of course, dear," Dr. McCrane said, giving his wife a helping hand.

"Maxfield McCrane," his mother shouted when she had regained her feet and her dignity, "you're grounded for life!"

"Er, Max," Dr. McCrane said in a low voice, "perhaps you'd better see your friends to the door. Your mother and I will discuss this matter—in private."

After their adventure, things were never the same for Max, Allie, and Grady. Max was grounded—not for life, as it turned out, but for a whole month—no TV, no computer games, and, above all, *no inventing*. He was allowed to read books, however, and that was fine with Max. He had a lot of science fiction books he'd been meaning to catch up on.

Allie, meanwhile, lost interest in books by J. Farthington Frimby. "Once you've seen a real dragon," she said, "made-up stories about dragons don't cut it."

Grady's mother was astonished at the change in her son. Once moody and unhappy, Grady suddenly became enthusiastic about life. He talked often about his father—not as if his dad was gone forever, but as if he was merely away. Grady seemed strangely confident that he would see his father again.

Max, Allie, and Grady entered Timebender as their project for Invention Convention. With help from Dr. McCrane, they took the car apart and reassembled it in the cafeteria at Victor Appleton Middle School. They wrote up their adventure and printed out copies on Max's computer. They also played Max's video of Allie and Grady petting the Stegocerases. A sign taped to the roof of the VW read:

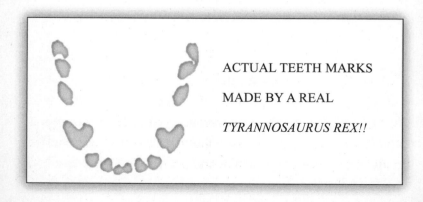

ACTUAL TEETH MARKS

MADE BY A REAL

TYRANNOSAURUS REX!!

The Invention Convention judges marveled at the "inventiveness" of their story, the "amazing realism" of their video, and the "added touch" of the giant teeth marks in the roof of the car. They made special note of the "whimsical notion" of describing Tyrannosaurus rex as a *purple* dinosaur. In the end, the baffled judges awarded an Honorable Mention for "Most Imaginative Wacky Contraption" to Timebender.

Later, when Max showed the award to his dad, the young inventor complained, "The judges thought it was all a hoax, Dad."

"You know, son," Dr. McCrane said, "I think it's probably just as well that nobody believes it. Let's keep it that way."

At the awards assembly, the entire audience was stunned when the grand prize went to Toby Brubaker's invention, the Automatic Ego Booster. It was a machine worn on the shoulders. When you pressed a button on the Ego Booster, a plastic hand patted you on the back, and a recorded voice said, "We're proud of you! You're the greatest!"

After the assembly, Max, Allie, and Grady stopped Toby outside the cafeteria. "We just wanted to congratulate you," Max said.

"Dude!" Toby sneered. "I don't need your congratulations—I've got my own." He pressed the button on the Ego Booster, and it proceeded to praise him and pat him on the back.

"Nice," Allie said. "By the way, Toby, we wanted to invite you to join our club."

"Club?" Toby asked. "What club?"

"Timebenders," Grady said. "Only time travelers are allowed in the club.

"And the four of us," Max added, "are the only time travelers we know of."

Toby laughed. "You guys never quit!" he snorted. "All that talk about time travel and dinosaurs and stuff! You know, I had a crazy dream the other night that I actually went with you guys and almost got eaten by a T. rex! Is that lame or what?"

"Toby," Allie said, "that really happened!"

"Yeah, right." Toby chuckled. "Dorks! You know what you can do with your loser club!" He scratched a place in the center of his forehead, then walked away laughing. A plastic hand patted him on the back as he went.

"Well," Grady said, "what do you guys want to do after school?"

Max shrugged. "Want to come to my house and invent something?"

"Cool!" Allie said. "What should we invent?"

"I was thinking," Max said. "We didn't see much of Mars when we were there. Wouldn't it be cool to go back?"

"Mars!" Allie's eyes widened.

Grady put his hands up. "Uh-uh. Nope. Not me. You're not getting me on some do-it-yourself rocket to Mars!"

"Who said anything about rockets?" Max asked. "Rockets are dangerous! Those things can blow up!"

Allie sighed. "Well, *that's* a relief!"

"But," Max said, "I've got this really cool idea for an Antigravity Machine. . . ."

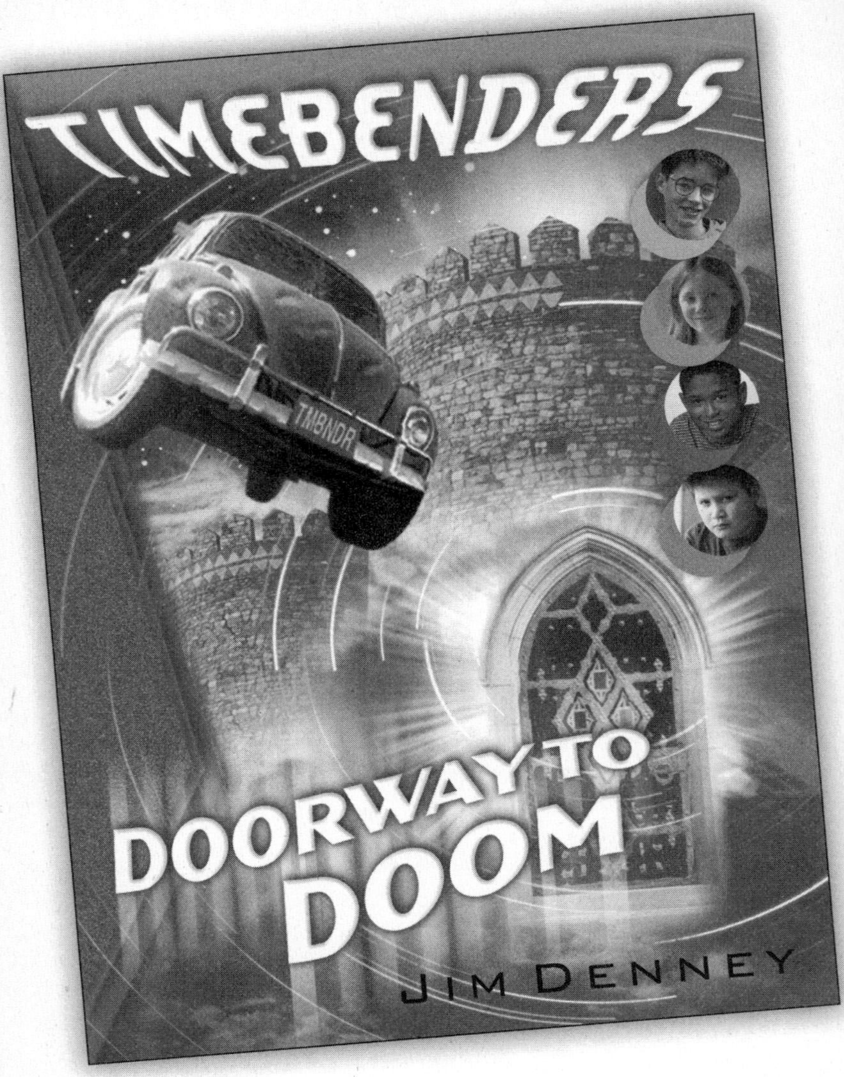
TIMEBENDERS
TMBNDR
DOORWAY TO DOOM
JIM DENNEY

Experience More
Time-Travel Adventures

in

DOORWAY TO DOOM

Excerpt • Timebenders # 2 • *Doorway to Doom*

Max walked to the study and pushed the door open. The hinges groaned. "Dad," he whispered, "would you—"

Max stopped. His eyes snapped wide open.

There was a man in the study—but he was *not* Max's father. He was over six feet tall and dressed in a hooded purple cloak over flowing robes of velvety black. He was old and had a long, gray beard; bushy, gray eyebrows; and dark, stormy eyes.

The man had been rummaging through the books on the shelves. A dozen books were scattered on the carpet. The stranger held a book in his hands and he looked up from it, directly into Max's eyes.

The strange man pointed a long, bony finger at Max. "Come here, lad!" he said in a voice like a creaking door.

For a moment, Max was frozen in place. Then he

slammed the door shut, turned the key, and pulled it out of the lock. The intruder was trapped in the study.

"Dad! Mom!" Max yelled, running to the foot of the staircase. Behind him, the door of the study shook and rattled. Max's heart fluttered like bat wings. "Dad! Mom!" he shouted again. "There's a burglar in the study!"

"Coming, Max!" his dad called out. Though it seemed to Max like an eternity, it was only seconds later that Max's dad came running and stumbling down the stairs in his pajamas, his hair wild, his thick-lensed glasses askew on his nose. Max's mother came a few steps behind, face pale with fear, pulling her robe on as she ran down the stairs.

Max's father reached the bottom of the stairs. "What's wrong?"

"The burglar's in there, Dad!" Max shouted, pointing to the study. "I locked him in!"

"Oh, my!" Mrs. McCrane turned to her husband. "Oswald, I'll call nine-one-one!"

"Wait, dear," Dr. McCrane said. "I'll handle this." He turned to Max. "Are you *sure* you saw a burglar, Max? You didn't just have a bad dream?"

"I really saw the guy, Dad," Max said firmly. His breathing made a wheezing sound.

"I'll get your asthma inhaler, Max," Mrs. McCrane said. She went away, leaving Max and Dr. McCrane standing in the entryway.

"Wait here, Max," Dr. McCrane said. Max's father dashed into the living room and returned with a fireplace poker. He turned to Max. "On the count of three, open the door." He raised the poker. "Ready, Max?"

"Ready, Dad," Max said. He put the key into the lock and prepared to turn it. His hand shook.

Dr. McCrane set his jaw. "One . . . two . . . *three!*"

Max turned the key, grasped the knob, and pushed the door open. Dr. McCrane rushed into the study. Max expected to hear shouts, threats, the sound of a struggle. Instead, he heard . . . Nothing.

Max peered around the door and saw his father in the middle of the study, the fireplace poker hanging limply at his side. The strange old man in the hooded cloak was gone.

Max walked into the study and nervously looked all around. He carefully peeked behind his dad's favorite over-stuffed leather chair and ottoman—no one there. Nor could anyone be hiding behind the antique globe, the carved mahogany umbrella stand, or the flimsy-looking William IV armchairs. The stranger seemed to have simply—*vanished*.

"That's impossible!" Max said. "He was here, honest! He looked like some old wizard!"

Max's father put his finger to his lips, as if to say, *Shhh!* He pointed toward the elaborate Doorway at the far end of the room.

The Doorway was the oldest of all the antiques in the old McCrane House. Max's grandfather had found it in a London antique shop after the end of World War II. It had been salvaged from a crumbling old castle in the north of England. It was so ornate and richly decorated that Max imagined it had once adorned the entrance to a king's throne room or treasury room. Now, however, it was just the door of his father's closet.

The door itself was made of oak with inlaid panels, warped and stained with age. The doorframe consisted of a pair of richly carved doorposts, topped by an elaborately carved lintel. The lintel and doorposts were covered in a thin layer of gold. Set into the pillars and lintel were crystals of clear quartz. Each crystal was about an inch in diameter, cut with facets like huge diamonds. There were twenty-seven crystals in all—ten spaced along each doorpost and seven spaced across the lintel. Jutting out of the doorframe on the right-hand side was a cup-shaped receptacle of blackened metal that, a thousand years earlier, was probably shiny brass.

Dr. McCrane gripped the fireplace poker and motioned Max to stand away from the Doorway.

Just then, Mrs. McCrane returned with Max's inhaler. "Oh, Oswald!" she said in a shrill voice, clutching her robe. "Please be careful!"

Max and his dad turned and gave her a *Shhh!* sign with their fingers to their lips. Then Dr. McCrane grasped the iron door handle and pulled. The door swung on rasping iron hinges. Dr. McCrane raised the poker—

But no one was there. The closet was empty except for some cardboard boxes and cobwebs.